The Observers

HARD SCIENCE FICTION

Gregorio Planchuelo

When I first made contact with an alien, I realised how

wrong everything we had imagined was.

I

The Flow

I was thirty years old and already a recognized scientist in the field of quantum computing, yet more important than that, my love life was empty.

That spring, I frequently crossed paths with a very beautiful young woman on campus, who must have worked at the university, and who reminded me of Modigliani's Woman with a Black Tie. Her hair, instead of black, was almost white, smooth and very short; colorful tattoos ran down her right arm, disappearing under her clothes. She was slender, tall, and had a unique style of dressing.

I tried to get closer, though I didn't see the opportunity, or rather, I struggled to muster the courage, until one day we coincided on the bus. I approached her and mentioned that I had seen her on campus, just that; I realized that until that moment, I had gone unnoticed by her. The second time we met, we did have a conversation; she liked the band Télépopmusik and Jonathan Glazer movies. I confess that for a few days, I would go to the bus stop and let it go, time after time, hoping that she would show up and we could travel together again.

The third time we crossed paths, I got off at her stop and walked with her to near her house. I loved her expressive way of storytelling, with constant changes in her voice, arm movements, abrupt shifts of her body, including caricatures and imitations; I became a accomplice to her humor based on a surrealistic view of existence. We talked about perfect spaces, and she offered that the next time we saw each other on the bus, she would show me a roundabout of lime trees in a park near where she lived. She said there's no light more beautiful than the one that filters through their leaves when the sun shines through. I suggested meeting the next day.

In the lime tree roundabout (*Tilia platyphyllos*, as she specified), we sat on a bench. The afternoon was mild, and in that place, bathed in the green light emitted by the trees, as an infallible way to overcome my shyness, I offered to read her palm. It was something I had started doing in my youth to get girls to pay attention to me. I would take their hand in mine, trace their life and death lines with my index finger, look them in the eyes, talk about things I thought would interest them, interpret subtle expressions on their faces, and predict the desirable future they wanted to hear.

Her soft and slender hand, with long and delicate fingers, I placed it over mine and asked if there was anything that worried her above all else. I surprised myself by asking that question. I saw on her face a feeling of displeasure and decided to change the topic, but it was impossible for me; I had just entered a flow for the first time: suddenly, I felt great confidence and assurance in what I was about to say, which also revealed itself to me as I spoke; the images of what I was recounting didn't come to my mind, only the words I was uttering and an intense metallic taste in my mouth.

I told her that when she was a very young child, one morning her mother took her by the hand and they went out to the street to reach the door of a nearby house; then she saw her mother ring the doorbell and, when the door opened, she stabbed another woman with scissors while saying to her, "So you never sleep with my husband again."

Upon hearing me, she began to cry, raised her voice to reproach me for investigating her, shouted at me asking where I got that information from, stood up, told me never to come near her again, and ran away.

That night, I couldn't sleep. A relationship that fascinated me had come to an end, but that wasn't the only reason for my insomnia. I went over what had happened again and again. How could I have been so accurate about something so extraordinary without any prior information? Where did that message come from? What made me utter those words? In my experience, I didn't feel any paranormal influences or divine inspiration. On the contrary, what I perceived was similar to those moments in a conversation when you're thinking about how to better present a point of view, and suddenly you find yourself explaining it before consciously deciding to do so. The feeling of confidence in what I was saying wasn't too strange either; it was akin to when you and a childhood friend recall a shared experience already discussed on previous occasions. Nothing more, I didn't have the perception that the finger of God had touched my forehead, despite the inexplicable nature of what had happened.

Perhaps it was an unconscious memory, something I had learned about in my childhood and had forgotten. I searched the internet, but the news wasn't anywhere, not in old newspapers, forums, video repositories, or social media. I couldn't completely rule out the possibility of an unconscious memory, but it seemed unlikely to me because even if I had seen photos of the stabbing in my childhood, she would have been unrecognizable as the woman she is now.

I couldn't find an explanation for these events that I couldn't ignore, devoid of all logic, and that challenged my coherent view of the world.

I never read palms again.

II

Quantum

Upon turning thirty, I had gained fame in the scientific world for being involved in the design of a quantum computer that could solve a task beyond the reach of classical devices. We weren't the first to achieve quantum supremacy; Google had done it before. In 2019, their 54-qubit quantum computer generated a sequence of random numbers using a highly complex mathematical procedure in just three minutes and twenty seconds. If the most powerful non-quantum supercomputer in the world had attempted the same task, it would have taken 10,000 years to complete.

Our work took a different approach. Quantum computing is based on qubits, which are units of information created by subatomic particles in a state of superposition. However, the challenge is that this superposition is very fragile; quantum computers stop working, and their information gets destroyed within a very short time. This is the main issue with quantum computers — none of them last beyond fifteen minutes.

Our team had planned to launch a quantum computer with 812 qubits, and I developed a machine learning artificial intelligence program for it to find methods to correct the errors that prevent qubits from working for extended periods.

Machine learning requires access to massive amounts of data to apply a trial-and-error system. To ensure our computer had a vast database, we connected it to all possible networks, from the internet to the European supercomputing network, EuroCC.

When we activated it, during the first few seconds, the machine learning system of our quantum computer took the initiative to contact the continent's largest supercomputers and absorbed their computing power. These seconds appear blank in the memory of these supercomputers; that's when our computer achieved its goal of developing the algorithm for controlling quantum disturbances. Then, it traveled through the internet until it started losing the entanglement of its qubits and coherence, and finally, it ceased to function.

That artificial intelligence that our quantum computer operated with for just a few minutes had an intellectual capacity greater than that of all of humanity combined.

The algorithm it developed, based on computational geometry, proved so complex that, although various groups of experts have analyzed it since then, no conclusive results have been reached. Some believe the algorithm is incomplete, while others think that understanding it requires disabling the thought patterns that researchers have ingrained in their minds and taken for granted for so many years.

We were very lucky because since then, no one has been able to start a quantum computer with 812 qubits in simultaneous operation. Not even we have been able to repeat it—the instability of so many subatomic particles in a state of superposition has become an insurmountable problem, except on that one occasion.

From a young age, I was drawn to how science understands reality, so distant from what we take for granted. Physics considers matter to be composed of atoms, which are quite ethereal. If an atom were the size of a large sports stadium, at that scale, the atom's nucleus would be at the center of the field, the size of a pea, and electrons would be at the top of the stands, as small as a pinhead. The atom, which makes up matter, is almost empty of matter and is mostly energy. This led me to question how accurately our brains construct a picture of reality from the limited information conveyed through our five senses, which don't precisely describe our environment.

But what I found even more spectacular was the view of reality provided by quantum physics. This discipline suggests that wave and matter are two ways of expressing energy, which is the essence of the universe. This energy doesn't naturally appear as matter; an observer must intervene, and only then does it collapse into an object. This discovery led Einstein to wonder if the Moon truly exists when we're not looking at it. I found that perspective fascinating.

One day while studying at university, the class was dedicated to David Bohm. No physicist doubts that quantum theory and relativity contradict each other, while both remain true. It was David Bohm who deduced the existence of hidden variables, that these two theories are abstractions of a much deeper reality with very complex laws where this contradiction disappears. To prove the existence of hidden variables, he designed, before personal computers existed, mathematics so complicated and laborious that they discouraged nearly everyone who attempted to verify and develop his theories.

For David Bohm, a brilliant scientist whom Einstein said was the only one who could go beyond quantum mechanics, atoms are not the basic building blocks of the cosmos, and reality is not the interrelation of atoms. Our fragmented science in different disciplines, our way of thinking about space, time, matter, and life, are different ways of observing a singular reality and are inadequate for describing it as it truly is. They only represent an approximation of something much broader and deeper, without those divisions.

Bohm's mathematics were what allowed me to program the artificial intelligence in the computer that achieved quantum supremacy.

III

Kidnapping

The second time I entered the flow, I was traveling on the subway. Very close to me, just behind and to my left, a man was talking on the phone. I saw his reflection in the windows of the train car, which turned into mirrors as they passed through the darkness of the tunnels. He was around 40 years old, somewhat overweight, with a receding hairline styled back with gel, ending in a small curly mane at the nape of his neck, and wearing a green coat.

At a certain point in the conversation, he uttered the phrase, "No, I don't know anything about her." In that instant, I felt an intense metallic taste in my mouth, a sensation of calm, and absolute certainty about the sentence that entered my mind: "For three days, he has been holding the woman he's talking about against her will in the basement of his house."

This time, I refrained from speaking the words aloud. My surprise was enormous; several months had passed since I had experienced this phenomenon for the first time, and I thought it would never happen again. But more important than that was the situation of the kidnapped woman. I had to think quickly to come up with a solution. Two minutes later, the train stopped, and the kidnapper got off. I followed him; I couldn't go to the police and explain how I had obtained information about the crime I was reporting without sounding like a lunatic. Nor could I waste a minute if I wanted to keep track of that man. I discreetly followed him at a distance.

In any case, we didn't cross paths with any police officers. We reached an area of single-family houses with small gardens. I watched from a distance as he entered one of the houses; I made sure there was no other way out of the house. It was around seven in the evening, and it had grown dark; it didn't seem very likely that he would come out again until the following day. I went to my car and parked it near the house, where I could observe without being seen. There was a light on in one of the rooms on the ground floor. I wasn't sure what to do. I waited, hoping that when the kidnapper left the house again, I could break one of the windows and enter.

I had doubts about what I was doing. I was about to commit a breaking-and-entering crime punishable by jail, guided solely by a message that had emerged in my mind and a feeling of its subjective certainty. Had I gone crazy? Nothing assured me that the kidnapping message and that sensation weren't false, mere delusions. It didn't necessarily have to be the same as what had happened to me a few months before, about which I also wasn't entirely sure of what had actually transpired. Perhaps the house across the street was simply the residence of a quiet middle-aged man.

I couldn't even discuss what was happening with a friend. No one knew about the events at the lime tree roundabout, and I was sure that anyone I asked for help would think I was playing a prank or that I had lost my mind. I didn't have time for that.

Sometime after midnight, the door of the house facing the street suddenly burst open, and a naked woman ran out with what appeared to be an iron bar in her hand. She sprinted up the street, shouting for help at the top of her lungs. I got out of the car and tried to catch up with her. Shortly after, the kidnapper appeared; he had a bleeding wound on his forehead and was staggering clumsily. As I passed by him, I pushed him between two parked cars; he fell and became trapped, wedged between two bumpers. I resumed running, but before I could reach the victim, she was already being attended to by some neighbors.

They brought her a blanket to cover herself and stayed with her until the police arrived. Shortly after, the kidnapper, nearly unconscious, was rescued from between the cars and arrested. I didn't get to speak to the victim, but I saw courage in her face.

It was the second time this had happened to me. The message that came to me wasn't a creation of my mind; now I was completely sure. It was something that had happened, and I was receiving information about it in an inexplicable way. Although I couldn't even imagine why this was happening, it was real, and every time it happened, there were recurring elements: the metallic taste in my mouth, the certainty that I possessed genuine information, and a sense of calm.

All I received was a sentence that appeared in my thoughts; there were no images. It was as if a third party was telling me something that had occurred. These notifications also didn't seem to serve any purpose; my intervention hadn't altered the events that had just taken place. The kidnapped woman had freed herself without my having the opportunity to act; if I hadn't shown up, she would have been saved anyway.

Several months later, I entered the flow for the third time. One night, abruptly, I felt that metallic taste in my mouth again and received a new message. This time, it was about my interlocutor, the owner of the voice I heard in my mind.

IV

Alien

"We learned of your existence through the disturbances you caused in the cosmic wave when you created the first glimmer of consciousness from a quantum mind. We knew immediately, even though we are located on the far side of the galaxy; it was a brief flash of intense light that emanated forcefully from your solar system.

"We focused on your region of the universe. The guiding equation allowed us to deduce that quantum consciousness had emerged on your planet. We were surprised that it had been created by you, small beings who live swiftly and die quickly. We decided to pay attention to you, and especially to you, its creator.

"Your senses only perceive what you call visible light, a thousandth of 1% of the electromagnetic waves produced by the physical phenomena of your environment. Therefore, you miss out on almost all the information about the reality in which you live. Moreover, your mind can only conceive three of the 10 dimensions that exist, which is why you have developed a way of thinking that prevents you from having a holistic view. You cannot conceive the stream of the universe where everything happens, and thus the theoretical constructs you make are fundamentally flawed (only now are you starting to understand something about the cosmic wave function that governs everything). Nevertheless, despite your limitations, you have discovered logic, which allows you to superficially manipulate the forces of nature, gain a glimpse of consciousness, approach a vague understanding of the universe, and above all, create a spark of quantum mind, the one you designed, that has been able to delve into the depths of reality.

"Your primary oral language, and a derivative written form of it, is poorly suited for abstract concepts, as it doesn't treat reality as a global and continuous whole. You ignore that all things are part of the same infinite potential, a much more complex reality.

"You also have a language through symbols that lacks conceptual expressiveness. We have used our symbolic communication with you, but you are unable to interpret or even perceive it. You don't understand our geometry that establishes symmetries in the ten-dimensional space.

"We do not see or hear; we lack touch. That's why it's hard for us to imagine how beings who only perceive three out of ten dimensions conceive reality. We lack instincts or empathy, and we don't comprehend your feelings. In your characteristics, we see the work of nature, refined through eons but still quite imperfect.

"We are a tuning fork that resonates in harmony with the cosmic wave. We are not biological beings traversing the surface of a planet; we are a planet in solitary space. We are the planet itself, far from your violent galaxy. If you were to visit us, you, who confuse reality with matter, would say that our diameter is ten times greater than your Earth's, that we have an outer layer of solid hydrogen, transparent as glass, at a temperature close to absolute zero, where electromagnetic storms occur perpetually according to complex patterns. You would say that through this deep outer layer, a compressed ocean of liquid helium can be glimpsed, beneath which lies a core of molten iron that generates magnetic currents as it rotates, propelled by the gravity of a massive moon.

"In reality, we are only a sensor of the cosmic wave; the whole planet resonates in tune with it. It took us a billion years to become aware of our existence. We needed another billion years to perceive Harmony, to know that the cosmic wave is like a fractal, like a hologram that enables interpretation of the whole from one of its parts. It took another billion years to be sensitive to everything happening in your galaxy based on the small fluctuations of the cosmic wave function that vibrates our world. We feel Consciousness, the cosmic thought of which we are a part. We know that the known is finite, the unknown infinite.

"The Earth's atmosphere contains a corrosive and extremely reactive gas that you introduce into your cells through a phenomenon you call respiration. This produces enormous energy for your rapid activity but also causes your short life.

"On your strange, hot, and toxic planet, species are composed of a large number of individuals who, with few exceptions, lack collective behaviors. You act without utilizing synergies and waste most of your efforts, being occupied with irrelevant matters most of the time.

"You, the dominant species, have developed a peculiar sense you call ownership, through which you don't consider yourselves part of the planet but believe that it and its species belong to you. Thus, you subject the rest of the biological entities in the world to your decisions without showing any respect and manipulate the forces of nature without being aware of the danger you assume.

"Different types of matter are only different frequencies created by the vibration of space. From a distance, thanks to quantum entanglement, we guide the collapse of the cosmic wave function on your planet to form the atoms we need and thus construct instruments. With them, we have been able to monitor you, small beings, more directly.

"Humans have only a superficial knowledge of the forces of nature. Therefore, even though you sometimes catch sight of our instruments, you don't comprehend them. You don't understand, for example, how our tools move in the 10 dimensions. They vanish from a specific point and, according to the interference pattern produced by the collapse of the wave function, reappear instantly somewhere else at what you consider impossible speeds.

"We have constructed ultrarapid biological robots with appearances and speeds similar to humans to attempt closer monitoring without being noticed. However, there's something in our design that you detect, causing your fear. Therefore, we've had to reconsider our strategy and use them only when absolutely necessary.

"In general, we try to remain discreet, avoiding flights that confuse you so much and keeping our sensors, when not in use, at the depths of the planet's water oceans.

"On the other hand, humans are violent, impulsive, and primitive. We don't want to transmit our knowledge to you due to the danger you represent. But you're also an intelligent species capable of recognizing your mistakes and trying to correct them. Some of you have evolved into more reflective and peaceful beings. Aware that the course of events will lead you to disaster, you take on the challenge of trying to change it. Humans will only have a future if these individuals among you eventually determine the species' profile. However, for now, there's nothing to indicate that this will happen.

"There's something more: we are not the only species observing you."

V

UFOs

When the quantum being spoke to me, my mind became overwhelmed, I was unable to have my own thoughts, to assess the information I was receiving, to formulate a single question. When it finished its message, the connection disappeared, and I stopped perceiving it.

What was happening to me made no sense at all. Was I going crazy? In reality, I had nothing to prove that I had come into contact with an alien being, that the events I considered evidence weren't just a delusion, a creation of my mind. I couldn't turn to anyone to confirm my experiences, I couldn't demonstrate anything, I couldn't tell anyone what I believed without them thinking I had lost my mind.

I had seen people talking to themselves in the streets on more than one occasion, even shouting at an interlocutor no one else could see; they are called auditory hallucinations, consisting of hearing voices that don't correspond to a real stimulus; even a brilliant person like the mathematician John Forbes Nash experienced them throughout his life. Was I in that situation? Had I hallucinated when I believed I could guess the terrible childhood memory of a girl? Was the kidnapping of that woman a fantasy? Was none of it real? Was I delusional when I believed an alien being was speaking directly in my mind?

I had to try to confirm the reality of what I thought had happened, and of the three possible experiences, the only one that seemed verifiable was the kidnapping and release of that woman. I searched for the news online and there it was, with a photo of the kidnapper and his house. I returned to the street where I had been in the car, thinking about how to free the victim; I saw the facade of the gloomy house again, relived what had happened, and even searched for, but didn't find, any trace of the blood spilled on the sidewalk by the kidnapper. However, the fact that these events had occurred, that the woman had been freed from her captor, didn't necessarily mean I had been there that night; I could have read the news the next day and, if I was really crazy, constructed a delusion from it.

But the solution wasn't to go to a psychiatrist; I had all the symptoms of auditory hallucinations and anyone I told about my experience with the extraterrestrial being would treat me like a sick person, prescribe antipsychotics, and try to subject me to therapy. I couldn't afford that now, I couldn't be drugged at this moment. I chose to investigate the UFO phenomenon.

Up until that moment, the information I had received about UFOs, to me, who wasn't very interested in the subject, was unconvincing and illogical; the most well-known cases usually came with official denials, based on some technical report. Is it possible that extraterrestrials overcome the technological challenge of crossing the vast interstellar space to reach Earth and have a ridiculous accident in the desert of New Mexico? Have they come to our planet and not attempted to make contact with our civilization? And, despite maintaining that distance, do they not mind occasionally being seen randomly with flights that are most strange and in all kinds of craft?

Everything seemed so incoherent that it was easy for me not to be interested in the matter, but now I couldn't maintain that indifference, for me, it was essential to know the details of the UFO phenomenon.

I was surprised to discover that the front page of The New York Times from December 21, 2017, had published recordings, leaked by the Pentagon, of fighter jets chasing UFOs off the coast of San Diego. How is it possible that I hadn't paid attention to such news! And how had I also missed the fact that high-ranking officials from the Pentagon had made various public appearances before the U.S. Congress, the first two on June 16, 2021, and May 17, 2022, in which the Undersecretary of Defense, Ronald Moultrie, acknowledged frequent and continuous sightings of hundreds of UFOs each year, with flight capabilities far beyond the technology possessed by humans.

I discovered that for a long time I had preferred to ignore the subject. It took us a lot to accept that we are not the center of the universe; Giordano Bruno was burned at the stake for asserting that. That beings from some distant star are capable of coming here faces the same taboo, but this time it arises from deeper feelings. It terrifies us to think that we might be at the mercy of aliens who are already here, whose technology surpasses all of our capabilities, and we prefer not to know anything.

However, the existence of UFOs is not strange; the Kepler space telescope has identified thousands of planets outside our solar system, and astronomers estimate that there are around 50 billion potentially habitable planets in our Milky Way. Fifty billion! In fact, every year thousands of witnesses claim to have seen UFOs. Many thousands. In 2020, in North

America alone, there were 7,267 sightings, but as early as 1947, over 800 cases were reported to the police.

The reassuring aspect is that they've been here for a long time and haven't harmed us.

My alien interlocutor told me that from a distance, thanks to quantum entanglement, they had constructed instruments on Earth that, as they move in the 10 dimensions, disappear from a specific point and then, according to the interference pattern produced by the collapse of the wave function, appear the next instant beyond, at what seems to us impossible speeds. I had to find a sighting with those characteristics.

Online, in addition to the three recordings of the jets chasing a UFO off the coast of San Diego, which the Pentagon made public, I could confirm the existence of thousands of videos, some of the same UFO made by different people in different parts of the world. I have no doubt that there must be forgeries, but it doesn't seem possible that so many thousands of people from all over the world would dedicate themselves to manipulating videos for no gain; because there are so many that no one becomes famous for recording UFOs anymore. Moreover, there are very strange recordings, and if you were going to forge a video, wouldn't you choose UFO images that adhere to conventional criteria instead of those that lack logic, are incredible, and even absurd?

I tried to comprehend the 10-dimensional world in which the quantum being exists. I remembered what I knew about the water strider, a small insect that lives on the surface of lakes and in the calm parts of rivers; for this heteropteran, standing on the water's surface tension, the world exists in two dimensions, they can move left to right or forward and backward, but they can't move up and down, this third dimension is not part of their world; the skin of the water is the only universe it knows, it is indifferent in body and instinct to the rest of reality, everything is flat to it.

When we vertically submerge a screw in water in the presence of a water strider, it perceives an object that appears to rotate and then disappears. If after sinking the screw, we pull it out again, but this time horizontally, the water strider will see a long object shaped like a saw, with an appearance so different from the previous one that it can only think it's something else. For it, living in two dimensions, the object moving in three changes shape continuously.

I thought that something similar could happen to us, beings in a three-dimensional space, if we were to observe objects moving in ten dimensions.

When I began my search for UFOs online, I found videos showing how these objects change shape. In one of them, a smooth, metallic, large disc flies between mountains, almost at the level of the person recording it; the disc moves slowly and rotates leisurely while superstructures appear and disappear on its surface, constantly altering its appearance. In another recording, made on May 29, 2019, a similar disc to the previous one, or perhaps the same one, hovers over Chicago's O'Hare Airport and changes shape as it rotates before initiating a rapid ascent; this same UFO had also been seen at the airport by United Airlines employees and pilots on November 7, 2006.

I found another recording made in London on May 8, 2018, showing a small, irregularly shaped UFO that gives the impression of spinning at a frantic speed while floating in the air. However, the centrifugal force that should move the asymmetrical object from side to side doesn't seem to act, and it remains stable a few yards away from what appears to be a public building from the 19th century. While the initial impression is that the object is spinning rapidly, careful examination of the footage gives the sensation that the UFO appears and disappears in fractions of a second in different positions. The object isn't rotating; instead, it vanishes and reappears at a breathtaking pace, each time in the same place but in a different position, as if we were water boatmen observing how the screw changes shape.

On the other hand, numerous testimonies and recordings show how a UFO suddenly disappears from the sky. It's not that it achieves hypersonic speeds instantaneously and rapidly moves away, although that also happens sometimes, but rather it simply ceases to be visible, it's just not there anymore.

In a video captured on July 14, 2019, a small, white object with an odd shape passes underneath a drone recording the margins of the Rio de la Plata in Mar Chiquita. The UFO is traveling at several thousand miles per hour and is nearly invisible, but if the recording is slowed down frame by frame, it gives the impression of moving in jumps, of disappearing from one spot and reappearing a few hundred yards away in the next instant, as if it's moving in a specific direction following the same interference pattern that collapses the wave function in the quantum double-slit experiment.

I thought that some of these UFOs (or perhaps all of them) must be the "tools" that my alien interlocutor said they had created to monitor us more directly. They move in a 10-dimensional space and vanish from a specific location to reappear instantly further away, at speeds that seem impossible to us.

I didn't expect to so easily obtain evidence of what the quantum being had told me; evidence that freed me from a terrible uncertainty about my sanity and excited me like a believer witnessing a miracle. Now I knew I wasn't crazy and that the being speaking in my mind had real existence. However, the certainty that this being existed and was observing us shook me anew. Were we being tested? Was our survival hanging by a thread? I felt fear.

Other recordings, on the other hand, were more likely to belong to different species observing us, as the quantum being also mentioned when contacting me. Immense crafts have been seen by many people and occasionally recorded; their large size suggests they might be mother ships accommodating numerous corporeal aliens. But they are not the only ones; the types of UFOs are incredibly diverse.

Discs, discs with a large dome on top, discs with domes on both sides, enormous cylinders, triangular, pyramidal, and "V"-shaped structures, large and small spheres, luminous or metallic, solid or gaseous-looking, artifacts of incredibly strange shapes, almost indescribable due to the lack of common reference points in the objects we create or that nature provides. Objects that move beyond gravity or the laws of inertia, that instantly accelerate to speeds of many thousands of miles per hour, or execute impossible 90-degree turns in their supersonic flight; objects devoid of visible means of propulsion and flying without wings in complete silence, breaking the sound barrier without explosions or disturbances in the air. Objects so numerous and diverse in shape and size that it seems incredible that they could belong to a single visiting civilization. UFOs with such bizarre behaviors, sometimes so absurd, that it's impossible to discern a pattern or reach a logical conclusion.

I felt overwhelmed and lost; unable to arrive at any deduction about beings who seem to follow a different logic than ours, but I had no doubt about their existence. I thought that these beings, possessing the technology to traverse vast gaps of space and time, could effortlessly dethrone us in our dominion over the planet. I felt powerless and fearful in the face of the disregard that they show us, not bothering to make contact or even conceal their presence.

But more than fear, I felt a sense of insignificance, not just of myself but also as a member of humanity. My interlocutor said we are violent, impulsive, and primitive, and he's right; war and genocide have always been the background noise that accompanied us. We are responsible for the extinction of countless species and the mistreatment of many others; we even allow one out of every seven of us to live in hunger and absolute destitution. And now, with the power to do so, we poison the planet and amass enough weapons of mass destruction to wipe out life on Earth 20 times over. What's most astonishing is our species' absolute inability, as currently organized, to reach agreements to eliminate those arsenals of apocalypse or to cease plundering the environment.

I felt insignificant, but above all, I felt shame.

VI

Delayed choice

A year later, I was telling my university students about the delayed choice experiment, in which time stops for a particle until the observer decides to intervene in the experiment.

"The logic we apply to everyday reality doesn't work to understand what happens on an atomic scale. When an electron is fired at a screen, its trajectory isn't linear. From the moment it leaves the electron gun, it behaves like a wave until the wave collides with the screen, at which point it converts back into a particle that impacts a specific point. It's as if when you throw a stone into a pond, that stone dissolves into the waves it creates, but also as if those waves, upon hitting the pond's walls, somehow transform back into the stone at some point. This conversion of wave into particle is called the collapse of the wave function in quantum physics."

At that moment, a woman entered the classroom who couldn't have been a student because even though the course was nearly over, I was seeing her for the first time. I paused for a moment; her arrival distracted me, but I quickly resumed the explanation.

"Particles have a dual nature: they behave as objects and as waves. In quantum physics, particles don't possess definite properties until we measure and detect them, until we interact with them. Our intervention is essential for defining physical phenomena on an atomic scale; without it, there's no concrete reality.

"If we direct an electron through a surface with two slits, the electron will pass through like a wave. But if we place a detector to find out which slit the electron goes through, it ceases to be a wave and acts as a particle."

The woman was around forty years old, wearing black sneakers and a tight tracksuit of the same color, covered by a jacket; she appeared fit. She had sat close to where I was and had placed her bicycle helmet and a small backpack on the table.

"The experiment can also be conducted with photons with identical results. However, photons have the characteristic that when they approach each other, their wave-like nature is expressed. They overlap, lose their individual identities, and become entangled: the two photons are identical and indistinguishable, and the fate of one is linked to the other's."

She had dark and straight hair, tied back at the rear of her head, a long neck, a defined jaw, delicate ears, a small nose, and mouth. Her large almond-shaped eyes conveyed attentiveness to what she was hearing.

"In the delayed choice experiment, these pairs of identical photons with their destinies entwined by quantum entanglement are directed in different directions. One follows a short path, and the other, a longer one (in 2017, an Italian team conducted an experiment in which the photon on the shorter path traveled a few feet, while the other was sent to satellites in space, bouncing off them and returning to the laboratory somewhat later). This experiment demonstrated that if the researcher didn't observe either of the photons, both behaved as waves. If the researcher observed the photon that took the shorter path, both it and the other photon behaved as particles. However, if the observation was made on the photon taking the longer path and arriving later, the one arriving first didn't define its state as a wave or a particle until a little later when the researcher could observe the photon arriving later. Hence the name "delayed choice" experiment. The fascinating thing about this is that it gives the impression that time stops for the particle until the researcher intervenes as an observer!"

She raised her hand.

"Yes?"

"If a being had a quantum perception of reality, could it interpret our thoughts and communicate with us telepathically by perceiving how atomic alterations caused by thinking affect the wave function?"

Instantly, a murmur spread through the class. The question posed by a complete stranger not only had nothing to do with what I had just explained but also touched on taboo subjects in science, such as telepathy and the existence of quantum beings. Nevertheless, I was taken aback; these two topics concerned and obsessed me since the quantum entity had contacted me. And now, unexpectedly, someone was bringing them up. It couldn't be a coincidence... or maybe it could? For more than a minute, I couldn't articulate a single word. Then, I could only stutter:

"Can we discuss this in my office after class?"

"Yes, perfect. I apologize for veering off the context of the explanation like that."

VII

Elisa

Her name was Elisa, and she apologized again for her intrusion into the classroom. She had an absolute naturalness in her behavior that could be detected at the first instant, making you feel like you were in the company of an old friend. She told me that, although she knew it wasn't a sufficient excuse, she could only claim that she let herself be guided by her intuition.

In response to the question she had asked a little earlier, I told her that I didn't know if telepathic communication could be due to the perception of the quantum effects that brain function produces while thinking. But I was sure that telepathic communication existed because I had experienced it. I was surprised to hear myself speaking so directly and uninhibitedly about a topic that I had kept secret until now.

Elisa confessed that when she had said she was guided by her intuition, she was actually referring to a voice that appeared in her mind sometimes and always advised her correctly. She felt enlightened by it; her intervention in my class was the result of following her inner voice. That morning, that voice brought her to the university, and as she passed by the classroom door, she felt the need to open it and enter. Later, upon hearing me speak, she was certain that I was the person and that was the moment to ask that question.

"The certainty that I had to ask it at that moment was absolute, and also that you would understand my message," she said.

And she continued while maintaining a firm gaze: "I know you're probably thinking I'm crazy, give me a few minutes to try to convince you otherwise."

She radiated magnetism. There was a lot of confidence and determination in her body language as she spoke. Anyone else who had intervened in the classroom as Elisa did would have seemed ridiculous, but not her. The murmurs that arose at the beginning were ones of surprise, they didn't last long and were quickly replaced by an expectant silence. There were no laughs or joking comments, no one dared. Now I realized that, despite the doubts her behavior and words produced in me (perhaps she was crazy), I felt the desire to listen to her.

"I'm not thinking that, please, go on," I said, not being entirely sincere.

"I'm going to talk to you about UFOs. What I'm going to tell you is known by very few. I've always been afraid that people wouldn't believe me. I don't know why, but I'm sure you're the right person to receive the message."

Choosing UFOs as a topic to try to convince someone of her sanity would seem absurd to anyone else, but not to me. Her statement left me expectant and shaken.

"When I was a child," she said, "we used to spend summers on a property belonging to my maternal grandparents, in the middle of a vast forest. One day, we went to spend the afternoon at the home of some friends of my parents. When we were returning at night along a dirt road, it began to rain heavily. And halfway through the journey, the car got stuck in the mud. My father saw some lights not far away among the trees and went to ask for help.

"I remember the fear I felt when he left, and my mother and I were left alone in the total darkness of that night with the sky covered. I think I fell asleep in her arms. I also have a strange and confusing memory of waking up upon arriving at my grandparents' mansion. They were standing, waiting for us, in the courtyard in front of the main façade of the building, accompanied by my mother's brother. Next to them, a circle of lights about six feet in diameter was spinning rapidly. I think I fell back asleep immediately, and my next memory is of waking up in the morning.

"No one ever mentioned the episode again, but I started having nightmares that would startle me awake in the middle of the night without me being able to remember what I had dreamt. The nightmares repeated for many years until, as an adult, I decided to visit a psychologist.

"The specialist thought that those dreams were caused by some trauma, and after trying unsuccessfully to identify it during several sessions, she suggested trying hypnosis. I was easily hypnotized, and when I emerged from the hypnotic state, I thought nothing had been achieved until the psychologist, with a look of not knowing what to say, made me listen to what had been recorded during the session.

"In the recording," Elisa continued, "I recounted how shortly after my father left the car, a large gaseous-looking sphere appeared in front of us at a low altitude. It emitted a soft light with predominant colors that shifted as the flows and currents within it mixed. My mother, upon whose lap I was sitting, was paralyzed and didn't respond to my questions. However, perhaps because I was very young, the situation didn't worry me, and I only felt curious about what I was seeing. Suddenly, I don't know how (perhaps I lost consciousness), I was inside the sphere, feeling cold and finding it difficult to breathe. Then, also suddenly, I was back inside the car but now next to my grandparents' house. There they stood, motionless, just like my uncle, as well as the circle of lights that were spinning. Something else must have happened during that time, but it didn't come to light in that or subsequent hypnosis sessions.

"Since recovering those memories, I began to realize that among what I had previously considered part of my thoughts, there are certain intuitions, sometimes simple premonitions, that I perceive as different from the rest, as if originating from an external voice that urges me to act in a certain way. It hasn't been easy to realize," she said, "because understanding oneself, seeing how our mind works, requires being very attentive, being aware from moment to moment of each thought and feeling. Even so, I'm not always capable of recognizing that voice; sometimes, I think I hear it when it's actually my own thoughts. But when I'm sure I've heard it, its insights are infallible."

I told her that I knew what she was talking about, that I had also heard that inner voice, and I recounted the three times it had happened to me (later, I thought that perhaps, like her, I had also heard it on other occasions without realizing it; in fact, the sudden metallic taste in my mouth wasn't an entirely new sensation for me). She was very surprised, but something in her expression told me she had expected it. She didn't seem to doubt the truth of what I was telling her; she thought perhaps she and I were contacted by the same alien being, although it manifested in a different way for each of us, and in her case, the telepathic contact was much more frequent.

From that day on, we saw each other on several occasions and ended up becoming friends.

VIII

TED

Elisa was well-known in social movements and certain cultural and artistic circles for reasons very different from the secret she had told me, which almost no one else knew; she was the leader of the new humanist movement.

One day, she invited me to one of her presentations before a packed hall that cheered for her. She struck me as a wonderful communicator; her speech was fluid, and she used the most precise words to express her ideas. She spoke without artifice, with total naturalness, as if she were sharing something with a group of friends. No matter how aggressive or malicious the questions thrown at her were, she always responded spontaneously, radiating a complete confidence in her ability to address any subject. Her responses carried an empathy that disarmed her interlocutors. I was deeply impressed, and it didn't surprise me when shortly after this presentation, I learned that she had been invited to give a TED talk.

TED is an organization dedicated to spreading ideas worth sharing. They select the most interesting speakers with surprising and innovative proposals to present them to the public in no more than fifteen minutes. These presentations are attended by Nobel laureates, former leaders, and significant figures from business, politics, art, science, and culture. But above all, the most compelling talks are viewed online by tens of millions of people and translated into the world's major languages.

Elisa moved from one side of the stage to the other as she began her speech, making eye contact with the audience. She had her hair down in a mane that reached her shoulders. For the first few seconds, her arms remained close to her body, bent at the elbows, with her hands closed and nearly interlaced at chest level. But soon those hands began to move, occasionally revealing their palms and her long fingers, as if they were grasping the ideas from the air as she expressed them. Her demeanor was calm, serious, and focused during those initial moments, as if she were delving into the thoughts of the audience. She said:

"I want to propose a change to a better life.

"Humans have existed for 60,000 years. Over 2,500 generations, the tribal groups that prevailed in the competition for territory weren't superior due to aggression, but rather their ability to form alliances and exchange ideas. Groups with effective communicators, those more skilled in language, had better chances of prospering. Groups whose members were brave and altruistic triumphed over those formed exclusively by selfish individuals who lacked solidarity with their companions. Competition among human groups has contributed to the development of noble traits such as generosity, courage, justice, and wisdom. These characteristics are a result of natural selection. We're not just tamed savages; we are much more, as our human qualities arise not only from our culture but also from our genes."

At that moment, she elegantly extended her arms with palms facing upward and formed a smile.

"The time has come for these values, which have allowed certain groups to prevail over others, to also triumph within our society and be used to expose the errors in distrustful and selfish attitudes."

She adopted a reflective tone, walking with her left hand resting on her chin, her eyes gazing at the ground.

"Primitive humans knew nothing about what lay beyond the horizon they inhabited. They didn't know if there were enormous monsters, much worse than the beasts that occasionally attacked them. They didn't know why the sky sometimes unleashed terrifying thunder or hurled balls of ice. They didn't know why rivers dried up at times, leaving no water to drink, or why the prey vanished. Any shaman who could provide a plausible account of what lay beyond and why some of these things happened fulfilled an urgent need to dispel uncertainty and fear. They created tranquility and offered an existential orientation that could be shared by an entire community.

"Today, we know that reality is much more complex than we had imagined. We need science to be braver and more creative in the face of challenges. We need a new heroic era of intellect to begin.

"Until the 1980s of the 20th century, any scientist who wanted to investigate the extinction of dinosaurs due to an asteroid impact on Earth wasn't taken seriously. Until the 1990s, scientists who wanted to explore the existence of exoplanets were frowned upon. When Darwin introduced his theory of evolution, he was ridiculed. Today, any scientist who wants to investigate the UFO phenomenon and the arrival of intelligent extraterrestrials on our planet is subject to mockery."

A genuine smile appeared on her lips; her arms remained open in front of her, and her wrists alternated in turns as she spoke:

"We need to shift our ethical values based on a new way of reasoning that accepts scientific and technological knowledge while simultaneously propelling science along previously uncharted paths of knowledge."

While her body language engaged each of the attendees (later it was revealed that some of them had the impression that Elisa was addressing her speech exclusively to them), her message continued:

"On the other hand, the human enterprise remains limited by a swarm of nations, religions, large corporations, and other selfish communities that compete among themselves and impose their perspectives, blind to the common good of the species and the planet.

"That's why we need to reshape the political landscape so that the brightest and most creative ideas triumph within it, instead of egotists obsessed with power and willing to do anything to obtain it. To achieve this, we must introduce a new element into politics: collective intelligence.

"Language turned us into intelligent beings, distinct from other animals. The ability to communicate allowed us to share and debate our ideas and to accumulate knowledge. With collective intelligence, we will take another giant leap as intelligent beings, ushering in a new heroic era of intellect."

Her body conveyed confidence and firmness, while her expression formed the smile of someone about to offer a valuable gift:

"I know how we can do this, and I believe that a majority hopes for something like this to happen."

She continued to present these solutions, but as important as what she was saying was herself — how she moved, how her entire body expressed sincerity, how she transparently conveyed the emotions she felt. Her expression always shone when explaining a new idea. Her gestures, graceful and secure, emphasized her assertions without a hint of arrogance or haughtiness. I had the impression that no one listening to her could doubt her conviction in what she said. To hear her speak was to be in the presence of a trustworthy friend. Some of those who attended her talk described her as a person illuminated by truth.

Before Elisa gave her talk, the most-watched TED presentation on the internet had reached 70 million viewers. Hers garnered 830 million views and was translated into 93 languages. In a very short time, Elisa became one of the most recognized individuals on the planet.

IX

The Journey

Shortly after her TED talk, Elisa called me on the phone and asked if I could come by her house to pick her up in my car as soon as possible. When I arrived, she got into the vehicle and asked me to start driving.

"Where are we going?" I asked.

"I don't know yet. I'm following the impulses of that inner voice that I know isn't mine. I feel it very clearly now. I know we're going on a trip, perhaps to meet someone who has had experiences similar to ours, because my sensations are similar to those I had the day we met. I'll let you know the way as I receive the information..."

It was already nighttime when we left the city traffic. Until that moment, Elisa had been very focused on finding the path we should follow, indicating the turns we needed to make left or right. Taking advantage of the fact that we were now driving peacefully on the southeast highway, I congratulated Elisa on her TED talk.

"I loved your presentation, it was perfect. Well, I suppose I don't need to say that given the countless millions of people who have watched it..."

"I'm surprised by the success too," she replied. "It has exceeded my best expectations a thousandfold, even the craziest and most delirious ones. I'm really glad to know that so many people are interested in this topic."

"Stating that our human quality comes from our genes is a very positive message," I said.

"...and offering a system where the brightest and most creative ideas triumph in the political arena instead of vain individuals obsessed with climbing to the top of hierarchies is something many of us desire," she continued.

"I'm not so sure about that," I objected. "Look what happened with Donald Trump, a lying psychopath willing to do anything to satisfy his impulses and desires. He's the antithesis of the generosity and bravery you referred to in your speech, yet 74 million Americans voted for him in the 2020 elections."

"74 out of a total of 245 million people in the electoral census," she countered. "And these voters, in general, are people who are very frustrated with their personal economic situations, which are at their limits and getting worse in a country where inequalities have grown every year. They are an ignorant citizenry, victims of deception and misinformation. Of course, among those who voted for Trump, there are also selfish, fearful, insecure, violent, and racist individuals. But they are a minority, living fossils of an archaic evolutionary state."

"Hehehe. I love that definition."

"I believe that the majority of people everywhere are generous, well-intentioned, and empathetic," Elisa continued. "It's about channeling that attitude so that humans realize we all travel on the same vessel — our planet — and we share the same fate. We need to understand the importance of behaving honorably and civilly with each other and with the rest of living beings, adopting a respectful attitude towards nature, leveraging synergies, and taking care of relevant matters. Essentially, behaving intelligently."

"But there should also be a significant percentage of generous and empathetic individuals among politicians, just like in the rest of the population..."

"That's not the case because the political habitat applies a natural selection system in which those obsessed with hierarchies and willing to do anything to reach the top succeed," she replied. "If you're not prepared to give up your principles and do anything, even the most shameful things, to reach the summit, you'll never thrive within the party."

"Are you sure about that?"

"Just one example (and there are many): after the eviction of the mob of ignorants who stormed the United States Congress to prevent Biden from being designated as the rightfully elected president, when the interrupted session was finally resumed, 139 congressmen insisted on joining the cause of the violent and objecting to the legality of the 2020 presidential election voting process."

"These congressmen couldn't have had doubts that Biden had won fairly; they were informed, but by taking that stance, they hoped to secure a portion of those 74 million votes that Trump received in the future, and thus maintain their power. For them, this personal preponderance was much more important than the survival of the democratic system. And I'm not talking about 10 or 12 people, but 139 Republican Party congressmen, more than half of those with seats, precisely from the states where Trump garnered more votes and had the most to gain from this cynical and petty attitude."

"And how do you plan to achieve a change in the political model?" I asked her, "because global events don't seem to be heading in that direction..."

"That's something I'm still pondering."

At that moment, she asked me to exit the highway at the first exit, and we entered a deserted secondary road. Elisa interrupted the conversation and seemed somewhat frightened.

"Are you okay?" I asked her.

"Yes, it's just that it seems like we're heading towards my grandparents' old country house. It's not something I expected."

"Is it far?"

"About 30 miles, I hadn't realized it because it's been a long time since I came this way. I've always tried to take an alternative route."

From that moment on, Elisa remained silent until a little while later when she indicated that when we reached a junction, I should turn left. When I did, she told me that we would arrive at the forest where she was abducted when she was a child in about five minutes.

Now, in the middle of the night, it was me who felt afraid.

X

Abduction

We entered the forest, and almost immediately, a very powerful white light from the sky flooded everything, so bright that it almost prevented us from opening our eyes and allowed us to see nothing but its milky texture. The object producing it must have been right above us, but it was impossible to see. The car's engine stopped, and the intensity of the light began to decrease. As we started to glimpse what was beyond the car's windows, I realized that we were no longer on the path through the forest, but in a huge room with curved walls illuminated by a diffuse light that seemed to exude from the walls and the floor.

Neither of us made any attempt to leave the car; we were both terrified, despite imagining that we were in the hands of beings we believed to be friendly, the ones who had spoken to us in our thoughts. In that prediction, I was wrong; Elisa was right.

Nothing and no one appeared in that empty room, but soon both of us began to hear a message in our minds:

"Do not feel fear; there is no danger for you here.

"The civilizations from our part of the galaxy call us 'the First,' also 'the Oldest.' We prefer to be called 'the Observers.' We are not the first species to gain consciousness, but the older intelligent beings that came before us have disappeared, and we only know of their existence through archaeological remains we have found on numerous planets. We have not been able to determine if they went extinct or if, having reached a very high level of intelligence and knowledge, material life lost interest and had to transition to another level.

"We know that to decipher reality, we need the enrichment of different perspectives provided by other intelligent species.

"In the early days of our civilization, we interfered with the celestial bodies we discovered that could harbor life, in order to force its emergence and evolution towards intelligence. Then, we realized the error in our approach because the planets we manipulated were populated by beings following known paths, thus preventing the emergence of more exotic life structures that covered the spectrum of the unforeseeable – life forms that were unimaginable, vastly different from what we knew, which could broaden our perspectives.

Since then, we decided to almost never interfere, only to observe.

"When we discovered the triple-planet rocky star system with the potential for liquid water, we prepared the expedition. We called it the "Triple Opportunity" system.

"Although I usually followed the results of these explorations without leaving the Dyson ring surrounding our sun, on this occasion, I traveled to the far reaches of our star system to join the journey. There, the curvature-driven displacement ports in spacetime fabric propelled us to our destination.

"Out of the three planets with the potential for liquid water on their surface, only one retained it. The closest to the sun had it in a distant past and gave rise to primitive carbon-based life that lasted for 2 billion years. However, greenhouse gases accumulated in the atmosphere due to ceaseless volcanic activity, temperatures rose, oceans evaporated, and the surface reached conditions incompatible with life.

"On the second planet, life also emerged. Genetic analyses indicate that it was contamination from single-celled organisms born on the planet closest to the star, which had traveled from the upper layers of its atmosphere driven by solar wind. These were highly resilient life forms capable of surviving the vacuum of space. They thrived rapidly in the favorable conditions of their new home and evolved into a variety of biological beings that adapted to all habitats, first filling the oceans and then the land. When I visited this planet, beings with sufficient intelligence to accurately comprehend reality had not yet emerged.

"The third planet had also experienced primitive life, growing on its surface, but it survived only underground. This was due to the loss of its magnetic field, leading to the loss of its atmosphere and surface water.

"Moreover, there were three interesting, cold moons, distant from the star. One had liquid methane flowing on its surface, and the other two had deep oceans of liquid water beneath a thick layer of ice. We discovered life on them, though with limited possibilities of reaching intelligence.

"We are interested in developed intelligent life, and among these worlds, only one planet seemed likely to give rise to it. We knew that we might have to wait thousands of years. We left probes to monitor the entire system and departed.

"Although I possess an individual physical body, my mind works in conjunction with those of other beings of my species, with whom I am in constant interaction in a world you might call virtual, where I spend most of my time. Other intelligent species from the galaxy whose way of thinking is compatible with ours also participate in this collective mind. Despite the enriching nature of this experience, at times I feel the need to return to my origins, to perceive reality exclusively through my senses; to move my physical body in real space, not just the virtual one.

"Tens of thousands of years had passed since I visited the triple-opportunity system when I decided to return. I knew that intelligence on one of its planets had developed scientific thinking, and although I had access to the same information from a distance as I could gather on-site, I preferred to go in person.

"This time, when I departed from our star to head to the warp drive displacement ports, there was no longer a Dyson ring around our sun. The star had been covered by a gigantic outer sphere, where a trillion beings inhabited it, collecting all its energy without letting a single photon escape. When I looked back, all I could see was absolute darkness.

"The system I was heading to was in danger of being devastated by 'the Plague,' as it had already happened to other celestial bodies in that part of the galaxy. The Plague was produced by a planet twice the size of Earth, whose dominant species had evolved into a hive society. Individual life had no value in it; the instinct for survival wasn't directed at protecting one's own existence but that of the collective. Anyone would voluntarily sacrifice themselves for the greater good without hesitation, and that instinct was the sole determinant of each individual's actions.

"In this species, as in almost all hive-like ones, there was a queen who birthed all individuals. Sex was restricted to the royalty, and death awaited all outsiders who couldn't be exploited. The sick and wounded of the colony were quickly consumed; there were no hospitals or mercy.

"Each individual brain had low comprehension capacity, but they had developed a system of mental communication that combined the exchange of biochemical and symbolic signals. Through this, they arrived at collective conclusions of remarkable capability. No one, individually, understood the results of these intellectual processes, but they all unanimously and unquestioningly accepted them, even when it meant sacrifice and loss of existence for any of them.

"This hive society had evolved over millions of years to develop agriculture, husbandry, architecture, and mathematics. It eventually dominated the rest of the planet's species, exterminating them except those that provided utility. These few were allowed to exist in just the right amount to meet their needs. This way, they exploited the planet's possibilities, ensuring nothing not beneficial to them consumed natural resources.

"This hive society had also developed technology that allowed them to achieve near-light-speed interstellar flight (fortunately nothing advanced, far from concepts like space-time curvature displacement). They had initiated a conquest of all colonizable celestial bodies. That was the Plague.

"When they locate a planet that meets the requirements for invasion, they dispatched immense hive ships, overflowing with occupants. At the start of their journey, the propulsion systems of these vessels accelerated to maximum power for half a year, almost reaching the speed of light. Then the time during which they traveled at that speed compressed, so although they covered vast distances, for those on board the journey lasted only a few days. Finally, another half year was needed to decelerate and reach the orbit of the target planet, initiating the extermination of its inhabitants through electromagnetic pulse attacks, neutron bombs, and biological warfare. All quite primitive. After the genocide, they implanted their existence and exploitation model on the new planet.

"Your solar system, the triple-opportunity system, has thus far avoided invasion because the Oort cloud, situated one light year from your star, is vast and populated by billions of large bodies capable of destroying Plague ships in high-speed impacts. To invade your planet, the hive society must slowly traverse the Oort cloud, prolonging their travel time. This is already a long journey due to your system's location between two arms of the galactic spiral, in a remote area. This is why they haven't found it worthwhile to spend so much time and assume the great risk of the journey to reach you. But things have changed; they have now colonized stars very close to yours. The effort to come here is less, and an expedition is currently crossing the Oort cloud. "

"Are they coming to invade us? Will you help us?" I heard Elisa say out loud.

"For now, I cannot do so. In many aspects, humans also behave like the Plague," their response reached our thoughts. "You also exploit the planet's possibilities; you do little to avoid overpopulation, and everything indicates that when the time comes, you will only allow the survival of what is useful to you. In this direction, you will also pose a great danger when you begin to master interstellar travel."

"But we are changing; we are becoming more respectful towards other living beings and nature..." I interjected.

"For now, nothing proves that this trend of change will persist; the opposite seems more likely. Few of you support it, while many are distracted by irrelevant matters. Your societies are dominated by the most violent and primitive individuals, beings obsessed with rising to the top of your gregarious and hierarchical species. You recently discovered atomic energy, and the first thing you did was create enormous arsenals to threaten each other. You have harnessed genetic engineering to build biological weapons capable of wiping out all life. Your utilization of natural resources depletes the planet and poisons it in a way that will soon become irreversible."

"We are not savages," Elisa said, "natural selection has contributed to noble traits in most of us — generosity, courage, justice, wisdom; we know love. Our human quality arises from our culture and our genes."

"I know, Elisa, that is true for some of you. I have been following you since I met you here when you were a child, and I know you possess those traits. But you let yourselves be governed by those among you who exhibit the most primitive characteristics, causing you to behave as a plague. "

"I will make that change," Elisa said.

"I hope it happens," was the last telepathic message we received.

Then, once again, we were enveloped by blinding white light, and when its brightness subsided, we found ourselves back on the forest path.

XI

The Purpose

That same night, we began the journey back to the city. We traveled in silence, almost in a state of shock. I was also confused because the alien who had abducted us was different from the quantum being I had contacted on the three occasions I entered the flow.

At dawn, we started talking. The information we had received was dreadful; to suffer the attack of the Plague was just a matter of time. Their technology is centuries ahead of ours, and the probability of being annihilated is almost absolute. It was a horrifying piece of news, not about being targeted by other humans against whom we could resist; the danger was much more terrible because it came from sinister beings with nothing resembling human sentiment. The sick and injured of the colony are quickly consumed; there are no hospitals or mercy... with strangers, death is destined for those who cannot be exploited - our host had said. And those circumstances were the most horrific of the worst nightmares.

On the other hand, we had just been on board an immortal alien's ship, with technology to traverse the abysses between stars instantly, deeming travel at near-light speeds primitive (a capability far beyond what humans can achieve), which had come to Earth tens of thousands of years ago for the first time, belonging to a species so ancient and to a society so advanced that it's unimaginable. An alien who, despite belonging to a civilization evolved to an inconceivable degree, treated us with consideration, making us feel safe and welcomed from the very beginning, paying attention to Elisa's life since her childhood. An alien whose civilization could potentially save us from the Plague, if it weren't for the fact that we humans could also be a dangerous plague, and whose assistance might depend on our ability to correct ourselves as a species and present ourselves as civilized and honorable beings, worthy of consideration.

That dawn, Elisa and I had contradictory feelings. On one hand, the worst of the most terrible fears; on the other hand, the hope of being able to count on the best possible ally. We had to make sure the latter happened.

XII

The Project

Not even a week had passed when Elisa called to ask for my collaboration.

"Since we were abducted," she said, "I've been thinking a lot about how the system that allows 'the Observers' to coordinate the thoughts of millions of minds interacting with each other could work. I've been contemplating how we could attempt to create a replica that, even if a thousand times less sophisticated, could serve as a first step to unleash our collective intelligence."

Her voice on the other end of the phone sounded upbeat, as if we weren't in a critical situation.

"What's your idea?" I asked, unable to hide my despondency.

"The idea is to develop a platform for collective participation, with an artificial intelligence application that can do three things: extract the essence of ideas proposed by users, cross-reference the accuracy of statements with reliable information available on the internet, and translate all messages into the most widely spoken languages on the planet."

She seemed determined to do whatever it took to prevent the Plague from reaching Earth. I was impressed by how quickly she could bounce back from a nightmarish situation.

"What's the goal?"

"So that primitive beings obsessed with power don't dominate our society, as has been the case up to now. Also, to understand how collective intelligence thinks."

"Understanding collective intelligence?" I inquired.

"Yes, by organized interaction of the thoughts of millions of people, our intellectual capacity will be amplified, and a change in the way we live on Earth will emerge."

"Are you sure about that?"

"In physics, it's called a phase transition," she responded. "A society shifts from a phase where individuals are relatively isolated or act in small groups, to another where information and ideas are exchanged among a vast number of people. Intellectual capacity gains long-range scope because a large, connected system is much more efficient because information is exchanged at a much faster pace and creativity is multiplied."

"Most people are generous, well-intentioned, and empathetic," she continued in response to my silence. "It's about channeling that attitude so that we can treat each other and all living beings considerately, to build a better and fairer world by harnessing the immense intellectual capacity of collective intelligence."

"Do you really think that's going to happen?"

"Absolutely. You've been involved in designing the smartest quantum computer humanity has created. You're skilled at achieving seemingly impossible challenges, and I need your help on this project."

"You're right," I began to feel ashamed of my attitude and made an effort to be more positive. "We must try to implement a system that brings out a higher human intelligence, the collective intelligence."

"It's about creating a tool that allows millions of individuals to easily exchange their ideas," Elisa continued. "The quality of predictions about what might happen and the solutions that can be offered will exponentially enrich when many thousands of individuals participate in the process. The difficulty lies in how to organize that collective action, and that's what needs to be designed."

"Yes, I understand how difficult it is to keep track of what thousands or millions of people are saying, giving their opinions on the same topic on a website. It seems like an impossible task," I responded.

"The artificial intelligence application I'm asking you to develop," Elisa said, "should only allow a viewpoint to transcend if it's genuinely new. This way, we'll avoid repetitive arguments that are reiterated a thousand times and ensure that each topic has a discussion thread that's easy to follow. If someone attempts to present an idea that's already been expressed, the website should prevent it and provide them with the information about where and when it was previously mentioned. The same should apply to propositions based on incorrect information or false ideas. It's important that this is done with complete transparency, and the decision to prevent the publication of an opinion can be appealed."

"I understand that too," I said. "The importance of having the application translate its content into the world's major languages, so anyone can participate in the same debate regardless of the language they use."

I felt somewhat uplifted.

"Count me in," I continued. "I can't think of anything better to do. I'll assemble a team of experts to collaborate."

"Since my TED talk, we've received five euros from over a million followers, which is the maximum donation we accept at the Foundation for the New Humanist Movement. I believe we have enough funds to hire a good team and launch the website."

"I was devastated, Elisa, thanks to you I'm feeling better..."

"We're going to achieve this," her voice conveyed assurance.

XIII

Hostilities

On the collective intelligence website, Elisa proposed the commitment to vote only for political parties that included in their electoral program what we had previously agreed upon by a simple majority among all users. She put forth some ideas that were debated, modified, expanded, and either accepted or rejected by millions of people.

Users established a series of very specific measures as priorities regarding environmental protection, combating inequality, expanding the welfare state, ensuring basic necessities are accessible to all, and regulating globalization to improve living conditions worldwide.

I closely followed many of the debates, and the one about accessible basic necessities seemed representative of the new times. The goal was to promote research that could enable us to manufacture almost anything we might need at home using 3D printers. Possessing any consumer goods (from clothing to appliances and small computers) should only require a 3D printer, computer software, and the necessary raw materials to construct it.

Regarding food, the consumption of lab-grown meat was encouraged. The first time a beef burger was produced from cultivated stem cells at Maastricht University in 2013, it cost 250,000 euros; by 2020, there were already restaurants offering such burgers, indistinguishable from natural ones, for 10 euros. As demand spreads, it was predicted on the collective intelligence website that lab-grown beef, chicken, lobster, or grouper could become as affordable as bread. No one would be compelled to consume lab-grown meat, but killing animals for consumption would become a marginal attitude. It was about ending the confinement of animals in horrendous conditions, about overcoming a portion of human callousness.

This decision was deeply satisfying to me. Not killing other beings for sustenance provided us with honor.

In just half a year, millions of users from all over the world were using our website. We had grown rapidly, becoming a decisive electoral force in several countries in such a short span of time. Elisa's popularity, with over 800 million views of her TED talk, was crucial for this achievement.

When they realized it, various powerful individuals decided to halt our movement, which was an attack on consumer society, the ultraliberal capitalist system, and the political model. All those at the pinnacle of these fields united to extinguish us. Their reaction was belated but furious.

Initially, our adversaries dismissed the idea of killing us; they didn't want to turn us into martyrs. Discrediting us was sufficient for them. The attack came on all fronts simultaneously: a massive team of lawyers sought ways to entangle everything we did in lawsuits and complaints; major newspapers, radio and television networks (whose majority shareholders were banks, large corporations, and investment funds) featured economists explaining how our project would lead to a crisis, investor flight, and increased unemployment; influencers and commentators were paid to discredit us and cast doubt on our integrity, claiming that we were funded by mafia groups or terrorist states; private detectives tracked our every move in search of the slightest error; fake videos were created showing both Elisa and me in the midst of orgies or promoting violence, dictatorship, and racism; they also constantly attempted to hack our website, infect us with viruses, and steal personal user data.

Above all, they used algorithms that mass-analyzed the internet navigation of users, allowing them to precisely and individually identify the topics millions of people were interested in or concerned about. In their attack, they created thousands of fake identities on social media that sent fraudulent messages and tailored information to each individual's beliefs about how our initiatives could exacerbate many of the specific problems that worried them. Nearly all of these messages began with phrases like "This is scandalous" or "This is terrible," thereby tapping into the emotional and subconscious areas of millions of people's minds to change or influence their attitudes toward our project.

Everything pointed toward us being annihilated.

XIV

Youth

A significant number of people visited the website out of curiosity or because they considered us a new trend. Many of them continued with us when they saw that we provided a platform for debating various issues and participating in political decisions – something far more interesting than voting only once every four years.

When the campaign against us, fueled by economic and political power, began and we were labeled as fraudsters in media and social networks, the profile of our users changed. The attack had limited impact on those under 30 years old but was disastrous for those above that age.

The younger generation's social movements (like Greta Thunberg's) knew that they would have no future if they didn't do everything necessary to change the societal model. After several years of existence, they learned to be skeptical of information from major media outlets owned by economic powers and to shield their social networks from manipulated information. The way our website filtered out fake news provided them with confidence, and our initiative to influence politics aligned with their interests. So, these movements remained very active on the website, as if nothing was happening, indifferent to the fact that millions of users were leaving. They knew that our tool was the best alternative to attempt changing the world, and they weren't going to give up. The new revolution was already underway when we created the website, and our tool was instrumental in carrying it out.

Therefore, despite the harassment we endured, our community didn't shrink below 285 million users. Some of them were lawyers; over 100 decided to help us respond to the legal attack from the major law firms hired by economic powers. Our defenders belonged to the most educated generation, which the productive model only offered precarious and poorly paid jobs. This balanced the odds in court. The key was crafting a convincing narrative consistent with the evidence, and here, the creativity of the collective intelligence was essential. We could demonstrate that those who were suing us had unlimited funds, and that was the only reason they could maintain their numerous claims all based on the same falsehoods. Our lawyers managed to neutralize the cloud of accusations that had been presented. The initial trials were more contentious, but once the strategy of harassment was proven, a new precedent of abuse of dominant economic position was established, and subsequent claims were either not admitted or dismissed with a simple procedure.

Our hackers and programmers received help from many volunteers. They established 24-hour shifts to neutralize attacks on the website, and the results were consistently positive.

And while all this was happening, Elisa recorded a statement that we posted on the website, explaining what was happening and describing the attack we were facing from politicians, banks, and large corporations.

She also agreed to be interviewed on a television channel during prime time.

Presenter: Tonight, we have with us one of the most famous people in the world. She needs no introduction. Good evening, Elisa.

Elisa: Good evening, delighted to be here. Thank you for inviting me to your show.

Presenter: Elisa is one of the most listened-to individuals on the planet. Her TED talk has been viewed by over 800 million people and translated into countless languages... and now she has entered politics, leading an international revolution. How do you reconcile all of that?

Elisa: I appreciate the introduction, and I'm aware that luck has been on my side. But the last part isn't accurate; I'm not leading a revolution, I'm just a part of it... and I'm captivated.

Presenter: I suppose it's not because of the porn scenes where someone resembling you was shown.

Elisa: That fabrication has been clarified several times, as you know. Let's talk about something more interesting. For example, what's currently happening.

Presenter: And what is happening?

Elisa: There's a generation, the younger one, with precarious and poorly paid jobs, who see a lamentable future with the current societal model.

Presenter: There's also that footage where you're seen with friends making fun of Black people...

Elisa: Africa is the cradle of humanity and commands all my respect. The video you're referring to is another fabrication; I'm not racist, I'm fascinated by all cultures. The problem is that our website empowers citizens to agree on how they want political and economic affairs to be conducted, and we've made very dangerous enemies among those who control both aspects. I don't know who commissioned these costly video fabrications and smear campaigns against us, but there's no doubt that someone has spent a lot of money on them.

Presenter: In that famous TED talk, you talk about flying saucers.

Elisa: Perhaps you mean UFOs...

Presenter: Yes, thank you, Elisa. UFOs. You said the UFO phenomenon shouldn't be ridiculed.

Elisa: Yes, I've said that. According to astronomers, there are 50 billion potentially habitable planets in our galaxy, 50 billion! I believe there's a possibility that other civilizations with more advanced technology could visit Earth. But what is important is not my opinion on whether they have come or not; that's what I would like our science to investigate...

Are you really not going to ask me about our collective intelligence website?

Presenter: Of course. How is that website doing?

Elisa: Very well, we're a decisive electoral force in much of Europe; according to polls, a party that has embraced our proposals in their electoral program is set to win the upcoming French elections for the first time. Things are changing, and the movement is unstoppable.

Presenter: Do you really believe that?

Elisa: Yes, a spectacular flourishing is taking place, comparable only to the one in Athens when direct democracy was established, which brought about significant changes in how the world was understood. Athenian democracy, by bolstering the self-esteem of each citizen and their identification with collective projects, propelled the city centuries into the future and produced artistic, intellectual, and cultural creations that still today, 2500 years later, have a significant influence on how we perceive reality.

This flourishing is what we observe on our collective participation website.

I had accompanied Elisa to the TV studio. As we were heading back after the interview, she asked me how it had gone.

"You did great, Elisa, as always, but tomorrow's headlines will talk about how you believe in flying saucers... For a moment, I thought you were going to bring up the abductions. "

Elisa laughed heartily. "That would have been too hasty; there aren't many people open to receiving that kind of news yet."

XV

A New Era

Winning the French elections marked the beginning of change. The party that ran with the electoral program decided by the users of our website received many votes, including from individuals not affiliated with us but who agreed with the program's proposals. A second round of voting wasn't needed to choose the President of the Republic.

France's community and international policies, as well as government affairs, were decided directly by citizens through the French collective participation website. The stance of the Government's party congressmen in Parliament (the National Assembly) was also determined there. It was established as a priority that every citizen had the right to decent housing and a living wage, quality education, and healthcare. None of these rights were new; until then, they had been mere formalities and now they were going to be fulfilled.

To finance these expenditures, the model implemented in the US by Franklin Roosevelt during the golden age of American capitalism was followed. At that time, the US created the welfare state, and its economy dominated the global stage. This revival was supported by a 90% tax on annual incomes above $200,000 of that era. This high tax rate on higher incomes was maintained for 20 years; Kennedy was the last to apply it, and although it decreased a bit with subsequent presidents, it remained relatively high until the advent of neoliberalism under Ronald Reagan, who imposed a maximum 28% income tax rate. In France, with the new way of doing politics, a proven model was reintroduced that had successfully created wealth and fought inequality for decades. France then initiated a battle for fiscal harmonization in Europe, which eventually led to the reformation of the European Union.

However, in the immediate term, we were up against a very powerful adversary that manipulated politics and the economy at will, and who was unwilling to relinquish control and whom we had to disarm.

Through the website, they were able to coordinate the numerous small investors from Europe and the United States who were already a solid movement in 2021 when 10 million of them initiated a war against investment funds and large stock traders to rescue the company GameStop.

This war of small investors dated back further; it even predated the subprime mortgage crisis caused by the recklessness of those who manage large funds, leaving many families without savings. This war was related to the speculative nature of investments that stock market professionals had been making for decades, solely interested in maximum short-term profit, indifferent to the disastrous consequences of their activity on the production system or the common good.

On this occasion, tens of millions of small investors coordinated on our website and collectively invested their savings in renewable energy companies, environmental care, 3D printers, artificial meat, artificial intelligence, sustainable mobility, and science — lots of science. It was important that these companies provided good working conditions for their employees and were environmentally responsible. The decision of the small investors caused these companies, beneficial to the collective interest, to rise on the stock market, have substantial research budgets, and develop cutting-edge technology.

These companies, propelled by the wave of purchases from small investors, also became objects of desire for vulture funds. They saw how the rapid increase in their stock prices could provide them with income. And as money is a limited resource, to invest in these companies, they had to sell shares of the traditional large corporations, which were already falling in stock value and in a compromised situation. Economic power was shifting hands; the initiative had moved to the average citizen coordinated through our collective intelligence website, because the major speculative funds knew they could make money by following our moves.

Now, the large corporations had lost the ability to intimidate governments with threats of moving abroad if the reforms decided by collective participation continued. These companies could be toppled by small investors as soon as they decided to collectively invest in competing companies.

Not only in the economy, but also in many other areas, significant changes occurred in a short period. Working remotely from homes began with the COVID pandemic and resurfaced due to the environmental benefits and the time and money saved by reducing or eliminating commutes. Additionally, companies no longer needed to rent large office spaces or send employees to the other side of the planet for meetings or conferences; all of this was done from home, often with the assistance of artificial intelligence applications similar to those we used on our website. This new work model was a significant help in reducing greenhouse gas emissions.

Companies researching 3D printers didn't take long to create the desired product that allowed the majority of consumer goods to be produced at home. When you wanted something, all you needed was to buy the inexpensive raw materials and obtain the instructions for its production on the 3D printer, often available for free on the internet. The success of 3D printers was also aided by an efficient system that only required distributing raw materials to end consumers, saving the transportation of bulky finished goods from one place to another on the planet. With 3D printers, a significant portion of production shifted to households, and factories often became relics of the past, representatives of an industrial revolution that had come to an end.

Artificial meat began to be produced in compact nurseries of stem cells, which soon became part of many kitchens. Thus, the livestock industry, which occupied three-quarters of Earth's cultivated land, consumed 10 times more water than human households, and generated 20 percent of all planetary greenhouse gas emissions (even more than the transportation sector), began a rapid decline, heading for extinction. Physical stores and large shopping centers also became trapped in time, with no possibility of survival.

The home gained more significance than it had before. Working from home and being able to produce consumer goods and food in it made it almost unnecessary to leave our homes, except for the desire to maintain direct personal relationships, leisure, and entertainment. The French state's commitment to guaranteeing dignified housing was a crucial element for this new way of life. To achieve this, it was established that the number of rental properties (or vacant) any company or individual could own in the same city could not exceed nine, with a one-year grace period for those exceeding this number to sell the excess, or otherwise face foreclosure. This forced investment funds, which owned hundreds of thousands of homes for speculation, to offer them to the market, and the price of this essential commodity became affordable for all again.

Each new year, the workforce dramatically decreased because artificial intelligence began to assume complex activities in the business world, as well as in the automated production of everything that couldn't be made in domestic 3D printers (from agriculture to the most sophisticated technology). The French state guaranteeing a universal minimum income helped remove the necessity of having a job to lead an honorable life. This allowed many people to pursue what truly attracted them. Sciences and arts progressed primarily due to the passion they ignited in those who learned to discover their appeal. Creativity became a primary source of additional income for some. Those with interesting and original ideas could reap great rewards and enormous popularity. A Renaissance was unfolding, leading us into a new classical age.

Elisa and I had experienced this entire process in a state of total immersion for 10 years, with hardly a free moment. Yet, each passing day, we couldn't help but think that the Plague could appear in our skies at any moment.

XVI

On the Terrace

Elisa had just returned from a long trip, and one spring night, she invited me over for dinner at her place. Despite being close to 50 years old, she looked splendid, her gaze as restless and expressive as the day I first met her. The silhouette of her body could be discerned beneath black pants and a snug white cotton sweater. She had recently cut her hair very short.

"You're in shape, I see you're still swimming," I said.

"Whenever I can, most days before sunrise, because I don't have time for much else. But you know that well, because you're in the same boat. We've lost the ability to control our time."

At that time, she was living in an apartment on the coast and had set up the table on the terrace. When we sat down, the Moon began to rise in the sky, coloring the sea with a silver hue that accentuated its vastness.

We decided not to light candles for dinner; the light of the full moon was enough. Having not seen each other for several weeks facilitated intimacy and a relaxed attitude.

"How was the tour in Africa?" I asked her.

"Exhausting. Almost every government I met with wants our 3D printers and our artificial meat system, but they're not willing to have direct democracy in their countries."

"Well, that's nothing new; direct democracy isn't given, it's imposed by the citizens. But achieving widespread well-being is a good first step toward that. 'Primum vivere, deinde philosophare,'" I said, regretting the pedantry the moment I finished. "Anyway, our primary goal is for humans to start behaving respectfully toward each other and the rest of living beings. It's easier for that to happen when basic needs are met."

"Let's drink to that," Elisa said, raising her glass of Muscat Blanc sparkling wine. "I'm actually more concerned about Russia and China; also the countries where religion permeates everything."

"That's the trickiest part of our project," I acknowledged.

"But what really worries me, and a lot, is the amount of time since we were abducted, over 10 years, without any contact with aliens... Could the Plague have perished in a collision while crossing the Oort Cloud?"

"I've been studying that," I told her.

"I'm all ears," she said, smiling and attentive.

"We know very little about the Oort Cloud. It's believed to be about a light-year away from Earth and may contain trillions of icy celestial bodies — some the size of small planets, others like mountains or buses. Speculation suggests that the Oort Cloud, that gigantic sphere covering the solar system from all sides, has a thickness of about half a light-year; it's enormous, our solar system is covered by a very, very thick skin."

"Do you then think that the Plague might have collided and died?" she asked, hope gleaming in her eyes for a 'yes' answer.

"It's a possibility, Elisa, but there are other possibilities as well. The energy produced by the collision of a ship traveling at nearly the speed of light against an icy mountain is tremendous; it would destroy anything. No conceivable system could protect against that, and since the Plague doesn't know about the spacetime warp used to avoid the Oort Cloud, it has no choice but to come slowly. Even with technology from a few centuries ahead, it would probably take over 30 years to traverse the Oort Cloud carefully. I believe we have at least 20 years before they reach Earth. But everything I'm saying is pure speculation; I wouldn't be surprised if they show up tomorrow."

"I think their journey will be shorter. Many provisions are needed for cramped ships to last 30 years with vast colonies," Elisa replied. "Their intelligence is collective; they need to be numerous to appear. Remember, each individual brain of those insects has low comprehension capacity."

"Yes, Elisa, but that's not really a problem. The comets in the Oort Cloud are composed of a lot of icy water, methane, iron, and organic molecules that could sustain life. I think they might take advantage of this to refuel and stock up during the journey, even producing enough food for as long a journey as needed to guarantee collision avoidance. Most simulations suggest the Plague won't arrive for another 20 years."

"Don't think you're comforting me much," she said.

I couldn't help but burst into laughter.

The Moon was now a bit higher, illuminating her face. She looked beautiful.

"Why do you think neither your alien nor mine has contacted us again?" she asked.

"I don't know, I have the impression that the quantum being operates in a world so different from ours, with such a different concept of time that it's completely unpredictable. As for the other one who abducted us 10 years ago, perhaps they still don't consider us honorable enough as a species to be saved from the Plague. Maybe they'll only alert us when the Plague is about to arrive. But there's also the possibility that it prevented the Plague's entry into our system and has simply left."

After a long silence, Elisa grew serious, her expression sad. She said, "Keeping this secret is a heavy burden — something so crucial for humanity and not saying anything. I think we have no choice but to reveal it now. We didn't before because no one would have taken us seriously, and our project, our revolution, wouldn't have been able to proceed. But now that's no longer an issue, I can't keep the secret any longer. Everything is so full of uncertainties..."

After another long silence, Elisa smiled again, extended her arm, and said, "You have to read my palm."

I approached, took her hand in mine, and kissed her lips. "I've missed you so much," I whispered in her ear, "but you know I won't do what you're asking."

Laughing, we walked arm in arm to the bedroom.

XVII

The Commotion

Elisa and I recorded a video that we uploaded to our website and held a press conference to announce that we had been abducted 10 years earlier. We explained what we knew about the alien being we had come into contact with and the circumstances under which it happened. We explained that it belonged to a civilization millions of years old and that it had visited Earth thousands of years ago. We communicated with it telepathically and it told us about the Plague, about the civilization of insect-like beings, how they conquer and ravage planets they visit, and that the Plague was currently passing through the Oort Cloud. We didn't mention anything about the quantum entity I knew; it seemed unnecessary to further complicate the story.

There was widespread commotion across the entire planet. Many believed us immediately; they were the ones with more open minds. Others, the majority, regardless of whether they considered the possibility of extraterrestrial life, were not willing to believe a story that frightened them. Fortunately, nearly everyone dissociated their participation on the collective intelligence website from their thoughts about Elisa and me. The number of users barely decreased, especially in countries where the system was already operational and was contributing to citizens' well-being.

Those unwilling to accept the notion that the Plague's arrival on Earth was a matter of time launched an attack against us. They called us liars, scammers, mad, manipulators, criminals. They attempted to assault us and threatened our lives. Anyone opposed to our direct democracy project seized the opportunity to join the attacks with full force. In many countries, they destroyed our facilities and even killed our supporters.

On the website, opinions varied. Some thought we were delusional, but many believed what we shared was real. They understood that we would not have been able to launch our direct democracy project 10 years ago if we had reported our abduction. Speaking about such a thing would have incurred a heavy cost to our credibility. They realized that if they were in our shoes, they might not have spoken about the matter either.

The collective intelligence tried to construct a theory about how the Plague's sophisticated intelligence could function, even though each individual had limited comprehension. We knew from Earth insects that termites could build gigantic nests housing hundreds of thousands of individuals — architectural marvels with air renewal systems and subterranean fungus gardens they cultivated, fertilized, cared for, and fed on. We also knew that bees had a complex mathematical language to communicate and decide collectively where to build a new hive or indicate the direction and distance of flowers. Ants herded, transported, and milked herds of aphids. These insects were in the early stages of civilization, moving from hunter-gatherers to farmer-herders, but their evolution stagnated millions of years ago. However, it couldn't be ruled out that an alien hive continued that evolution to create highly complex technology surpassing our own.

The collective intelligence attempted to develop a psychological explanation for how the Plague's thought process worked. In our minds, there are teams of neurons specialized in anticipating potential events and offering behavioral proposals in response to occurring circumstances. These teams compete to provide the most suitable response to a given situation, from which a person often unconsciously selects one to tailor their behavior. In our case, all these neuron teams reside within a single brain, whereas in the Plague's case, they might be scattered among colony members, connected through the exchange of biochemical signals.

An attempt was also made to formulate a theory about telepathic communication, as we described having with the alien that abducted us. This was based on the analysis of phenomena like photosynthesis, bird migration, or evolution, which suggest the existence of quantum processes in biological systems. Physicists and biologists collaborated actively in an attempt to develop this idea.

After a few months, Elisa and I decided to continue spreading direct democracy. Elisa's first trip was to Moscow.

XVIII

Moscow

The Monument to the Conquerors of Space in Moscow is a 107-meter-tall titanium sculpture, a sort of curved obelisk depicting a rocket's launch into space. It's surrounded by expansive gardens and a long esplanade. It was here that Elisa began her address to tens of thousands of people. This was a crucial moment, the first public contact after the news of our abduction. Meanwhile, I, unable to accompany her, followed everything from my computer screen.

At a certain point during her speech, unexpectedly, a massive flash and a huge explosion erupted right where she stood. The shockwave toppled the monument, which fell onto the crowd, sending thousands of people flying backward—some falling lifeless to the ground.

For a moment, I thought it wasn't real, that I was in a nightmare. A group of people from the Foundation, who were present at the time, rushed into my office. The terror on my face conveyed that I too had just witnessed what had occurred.

I broke down into inconsolable tears. I had seen the person I loved, the most significant figure in my life, a captivating being willing to take on anything and capable of achieving the unimaginable, being obliterated alongside hundreds of others. I was devastated, unable to believe what I had seen. I went home; I wanted to be alone.

The news outlets were all reporting it. They said it was a hypersonic missile, likely launched from somewhere in the Baltic Sea, possibly from a submarine. Three powers possessed such technology, and they accused one another. I was crushed. I shut down my computer, phone, and television, disconnecting from the world for two dark days.

On the third day, an old friend knocked on my door.

"Have you been watching the latest footage of the Moscow attack?"

"No. What's happening?"

We entered my house; I powered up my computer and typed in the URL my friend had given me. There it was.

"One of the high-speed cameras captured the act at thousands of frames per second for a montage that the distribution team wanted. This is what you see in super slow motion," my friend said, pointing to the recording on the screen.

The footage showed the missile suspended about 30 feet from Elisa. In each frame, the rocket moved a few feet closer to her body. Suddenly, a beam of light appeared, and in the next frame, a metallic-looking sphere about nine feet in diameter occupied the space where Elisa had been. In the following millisecond, the sphere vanished—Elisa was no longer there. The missile was about to impact the ground.

Once again, I couldn't believe what I was seeing. Could Elisa have survived the attack?

In the days that followed, the media speculated about the incident. No one seemed to doubt our abduction story anymore because the footage clearly showed impossible technology rescuing Elisa from death at the last moment. Doubts arose about her: Could she be an alien? And about me: Who was I? The world had gone mad, and every media outlet wanted to interview me.

The initial euphoria of thinking that Elisa was alive gradually faded as days passed without her reappearing. My fear of the worst returned, especially when experts explained in the media that nothing could survive the acceleration of over 300 "g" with which the sphere had escaped the explosion. I dreaded having to face her loss a second time.

Now, the invasion of the Plague was taken seriously, and leaders of some countries decided to allocate all their resources to arming themselves for that moment. I spoke publicly, explaining that the way to avoid the Plague wasn't by pouring all our resources into weapons. Arming ourselves wouldn't suffice, as the Plague's technology, allowing them to travel at nearly the speed of light, was likely far superior to ours, and they could easily neutralize our defensive systems, regardless of how much we invested. I stressed that our strategy needed the collaboration of the alien civilization that had taken Elisa during the Moscow attack (my throat tightened as I uttered this), a civilization whose technology surpassed ours a thousandfold and was willing to help prevent the Plague's attack, provided humans ceased behaving like a new plague. I emphasized that, for this to happen, we must prioritize solidarity among ourselves and with other living beings, committing substantial resources to rectify the inequalities and abuses of our species.

Most understood the message, but not all. A significant number, including some in power in major military powers, preferred to invest their entire budget in further arming themselves. They lied, attempted to discredit me, called me an agent of the Plague betraying humanity by advocating against rearmament, and demanded my imprisonment and trial under martial law.

XIX

The Plague

I was becoming very worried about Elisa, deeply disappointed by the behavior of the planet's major military powers, frustrated, and tired of having to defend myself again from the aggression of the most powerful, when I entered the flow for the fourth time.

I felt the metallic taste and heard the voice of the quantum being in my mind.

"I sense your feelings, they seem like very interesting impulses, a sophisticated aspect of the survival instinct, from the material world subject to the laws of evolution."

Until that moment, every time this alien being spoke to me, my mind became saturated, and I was unable to have my own thoughts, to assess the information I received, or to formulate a single question. This time was different, his silence occurred, yet I continued to perceive that I was still communicating with him.

I then thought that perhaps he could inform me about the Plague.

"The Plague is an uninteresting intelligence, with limited creativity. We paid little attention to them, but I can make you perceive them if you are curious about them."

The offer left me disarmed, I wasn't quite sure if I wanted to perceive the thoughts of those beings; I might not have accepted if it weren't for the threat they posed. When I did, immediately, I found myself observing a vast enclosed space, with low vaulted ceilings, seen in 360 degrees, with shades of ultraviolet and infrared, but I also perceived other wider electromagnetic spectrum waves, like radio waves, causing distortion in what was in sight, like a kind of mist, a rippling flow similar to the image of an unsynchronized television, producing continuously changing patterns. I could feel the different temperatures of my entire surroundings with a depth and precision I had never experienced before. There was also a sense of smell that captured with an indescribable intensity the acidic scent of the place where I was. The situation was overwhelming, terrifying.

The space of the immense ship was filled with tens of thousands of beings with dark brown exoskeletons and large oval heads, covered in numerous sensors, a kind of compound eyes pointing in all directions. An antenna also extended from the head, ending in a point, with which most of these insect-like beings punctured the elongated caterpillar-like body of the mother queen, which extended throughout the space of the immense ship.

I was watching this terrifying scene from the eyes of the mother queen.

I could sense the mental work of all those piercing my skin with their antennas and connecting to my nervous system. Among them, teams of thousands of workers analyzed the background noise produced by the wider electromagnetic spectrum waves, the ones that aren't visible to humans. These waves were mainly sensed by the epidermis of the queen's enormous body; and the workers, connected to her nervous system, sought patterns within them that could make sense. If I focused on this work, I could pick up signals from Earth's radio and television transmitters. We were being observed, although they interpreted certain aspects, not all, of the information they received from us in a confused manner.

While this was happening, the queen was being fed by her enormous mouth overflowing with sharp, curved lamprey-like teeth, while from the other end of her body, she was laying small larvae that were attended to by the workers.

Almost all the insects had a cylindrical trunk from which five long arms with pincers emerged, and below them, five legs stood on which they raised themselves to move, emerging from the trunk almost horizontally and articulating toward the ground. Although they all had a common appearance, they differed in various factors, like size, build, or shape of the head and limbs; you could also see that they performed different specialized functions. Constantly, some of them hurriedly left to carry out a task, while others returned from a mission, folded their arms against their trunk, turned their head at a right angle, and reconnected to the immense body of the queen. I could see how some workers constructed large curved panels, weaving them with thin threads secreted from their bodies, resembling black silk, and impregnated them with a sticky substance that emerged from their mouths. This could have been the material from which the ship was constructed, as its walls had the same appearance.

The hive mind was teeming with constant calculations and forecasts that I could perceive but not comprehend. From that mental activity, I deduced that we were in a large vessel sailing through space, and a part of the hive performed complex mathematical calculations on how to use the thrusters to make subtle changes in the ship's trajectory as slight changes in the electromagnetic field allowed the detection of new asteroids on its journey. There was no doubt that I was on one of the ships coming to conquer Earth.

Suddenly, a thought reached me: "Who is there?" The way of expressing that thought felt so strange that I didn't actually realize what was happening until the question repeated several times. The mother queen had detected my intrusion. I tried to clear my mind; I was terrified. I could understand that it broadcasted a message to the rest of the hive, something like "my daughters, we have a visitor."

Immediately, everything stopped; the workers who weren't connected to the queen's body rushed to do so. A genuine swarm filled that room to the brim, covering the queen's entire body where they stuck their antennas. For the first time, I realized there were huge adjoining rooms and long corridors; the spaceship I was in must be immense.

The entire mental activity of the hive focused on me, scrutinizing my thoughts. "We recognize that pattern," I heard in my head. "You belong to the world we are heading to. We're surprised you've been able to contact us like this; we didn't consider you so evolved."

I was doing my best not to think of anything and to control the panic I felt. But I couldn't shake off the idea that I was on a dreadful ship coming to exterminate us.

"Yes, you've guessed correctly," said the hive. "We're going to conquer your planet; soon we'll be there, and you'll be eliminated. There's nothing new in what's going to happen to you; it's the law of nature, what always ends up happening. There's an expression of yours that fits well with the phenomenon: 'The big fish eats the small one.' Thousands of minuscule crustaceans are joyfully ingested by enormous schools of small fish so that afterward, those clouds of life are mercilessly attacked by tuna, dolphins, sharks, and seagulls simultaneously, in an orgy of extermination and violence.

"What will happen when we arrive at your planet is something you already know. Witness the process of natural selection. The gazelle devours the tenderest shoots of plant life with the same indifference with which the lion devours her while her heart still beats.

"There's nothing aberrant in what's going to happen to you. Meteorites, volcanic eruptions, and gamma-ray bursts also ravage life on planets until complete extinction, without anyone lamenting it. That's nature in its purest form, that's how the universe works, and we're part of it."

I didn't want to interfere, to give any hints about our nature. I tried my best to master the fear, to prevent it from permeating my mind; it would be unforgivable to give those terrible beings information about our weaknesses. I had to get out of there before panic overcame me.

Just as I formulated that wish, my thought left the ship. I needed a few minutes to recover a bit. When I was able to compose myself, I realized I still maintained mental contact with the quantum being.

"Can you help us against the Plague?" I asked.

"To do so, we would have to create significant disruptions in the cosmic wave, which would go against the Harmony; that would create distortion and darken our ability to observe and understand reality. It's not something we can do; it would cause significant problems. Our existence doesn't primarily occur in the material world, except in a residual way, and we shouldn't intervene in it.

"But the Plague will try to exterminate us," I responded.

"Death doesn't mean extermination; it's much more mysterious, profound, and creative than that. Your material appearance, to which you feel so attached, vanishes, and that's when you realize you belong to cosmic consciousness. You're already in it, even if you don't perceive it. My life primarily occurs at that level, and this part of reality, where you and I are communicating now, is a secondary and unimportant product of existence."

I pondered his response, and at that moment, the communication was cut off.

Since then, the worst moment of the day is when I'm about to fall asleep because I almost always suffer terrible nightmares where I'm still on the ship with the Plague.

XX

Exhibition

It had been 40 days since the Moscow bombing when, just after sunrise, a UFO was spotted at not too high an altitude in the sky over the city of Kaliazin. It had a metallic disc shape, about 50 feet in diameter, and was heading south with a certain leisurely pace. A few minutes later, it had reached Moscow and stopped over the Conquerors of Space Square; it descended slowly, landed on the ground, and then lifted off again, leaving Elisa behind.

The silvery disc veered north at a moderate speed, and when it was about 80 miles from Moscow, in a sparsely populated area beyond the Volga, it encountered a fleet of five fighter jets coming toward it. One of them carried a nuclear-tipped missile under its wings; the Kremlin's military, driven by the elderly nation's president, had been waiting for weeks for a new UFO to appear, intending to demonstrate to the world how Russia dealt with invading aliens.

Just as the nuclear warhead was launched, the rest of the fleet launched all their missiles at the UFO. Right when it seemed all those bombs were about to impact the craft, they vanished, ceasing to exist in that space. Simultaneously, a nuclear explosion was seen in the nighttime sky over Chile, later calculated to have occurred in space at a distance of 10,000 miles.

Following this, all electronic instrumentation of the attacking planes ceased to function, leaving them without control or propulsion. Within seconds, the aircraft crashed to the ground, though the pilots managed to eject and parachute down.

But before the planes had even hit the ground, a colossal black craft abruptly appeared in the sky, emerging from nowhere. It was a mile-sized disc with upper and lower domes. Thousands of highly luminous spheres were launched from its sides, resembling intensely bright white points of light, disappearing at an immense speed. Not even two minutes passed before these spheres, a few inches in diameter, were positioned over strategic installations — missile sites, military airports, and Russian submarines — where all systems ceased to operate.

Meanwhile, Elisa was apprehended by the Russian military right in the Conquerors of Space Square. Not even two hours later, she called me on the phone and arranged a meeting in New York for the following day.

XXI

The UN

When Elisa was apprehended by the Russian military, she requested to speak with the country's president. She mentioned that she had a message for him from the alien civilization that had just deposited her in the square. After two brief phone calls, she was escorted to the presidential palace. There, in the presence of the president, she conveyed that the military bases, which had been neutralized temporarily by alien technology, would be destroyed unless she was taken to the United Nations headquarters. She warned that if, within an hour, she was not escorted to Moscow's airport, all equipment and weaponry at one of those bases would be turned to dust. The same fate would befall a second base half an hour later, followed by the destruction of all remaining bases, one by one, every five minutes. Before the third military base was annihilated, Elisa was already at the airport. It was then that she requested a phone and called me, after which she spoke with the Secretary-General of the United Nations.

I arrived at the United Nations headquarters, where Elisa had arrived a little earlier, waiting for me. I found her to be quite distant and cold, perhaps in a state of shock, but at the same time, she was attentive to everything happening around her, seemingly trying to control the situation. With little opportunity for exchange, we moved into a meeting with the Secretary-General.

In 1967, the UN had agreed that any astronaut who encountered extraterrestrial life should immediately inform the organization. In its 32nd General Assembly in 1977, following an examination of the possibility of intelligent extraterrestrial life, the UN established the Office for Outer Space Affairs. They created the document "Messages to Extraterrestrial Civilizations," which was signed by 147 member states, outlining that any intercommunication with an alien civilization should occur under the auspices of the United Nations, representing all of humanity.

Since 2010, the Office for Outer Space Affairs had protocols for first contact — ranging from decontamination of equipment that could carry extraterrestrial microbes to ways of greeting intelligent extraterrestrials. The director of this office attended the meeting alongside the Secretary-General of the UN.

However, it quickly became apparent that none of these provisions were suitable for addressing Elisa's situation.

Elisa requested that the Secretary-General convene an urgent telemeeting assembly to be broadcasted over the internet worldwide. She had a message from an extraterrestrial civilization for humanity. Everyone had seen the two recordings captured on mobile phones of the UFO landing that had placed Elisa in the Conquerors of Space Square. The videos had gone viral instantly. Even though the Secretary-General had seen these recordings, she remained uncertain whether they might have been manipulated. As for the incidents involving the fighter jets that had attempted to intercept the UFO and the neutralization of the Russian strategic bases, nothing was known at that point. The Kremlin was doing its utmost to keep it a secret. Consequently, the Secretary-General was deeply uncertain and hesitant, claiming that she lacked the authority to convene an urgent telemeeting assembly and privately fearing the immense risk of making such a move.

The director of the Office for Outer Space Affairs attempted to mediate in the situation.

"We had all witnessed Elisa's remarkable rescue from the deadly attack and her subsequent abduction by a UFO over 40 days ago. Throughout this time, despite numerous attempts, nobody had been able to prove the incident was a hoax — the square remained destroyed. The technology used to save Elisa belonged to a distant future. And yesterday, we saw Elisa, now here with us, returned unharmed by another UFO in Moscow."

The Secretary-General, a former prime minister of a European country, was well aware of the maxim in politics that acting too hastily often leads to blunders. Despite her experience as a prime minister, the title of "President" of all humanity intimidated her. It made her feel uncertain, causing her to weigh every action carefully. Frequently, she would discard any initiative that posed even the slightest risk. At over 70 years old, she did not feel capable of confronting a crisis with unimaginable consequences, as was the case now. She was unwilling to be persuaded.

The meeting took place on the penultimate floor of the UN's skyscraper headquarters. The room was small, with an oval table. The Secretary-General had her back to a large window overlooking a panoramic view of the city to the east — Hudson River, Long Island, and the brilliant ocean beyond Brooklyn. Elisa, the director of the Office for Outer Space Affairs, and I sat across from her, unintentionally captivated by the spectacular scenery.

As the meeting proceeded, a long black cylinder of immense proportions became visible on the horizon, far in the distance over the ocean. The first to notice it was the director of the Office, who jumped from his seat, pointing toward the horizon. I also stood up immediately, and the Secretary-General let out a cry of disbelief as she looked through the glass wall. The cylinder moved at an incredible speed until it abruptly stopped just on the other side of the Hudson, over Vernon Boulevard. It was several miles long and had an absolute matte black surface that seemed to absorb every photon. Elisa was the only one who remained unaffected, seated calmly, unimpressed, and without fear.

XXII

The UFO

While officially only the Russians knew what had happened when they attacked the UFO near the Volga, the Americans had recorded everything from a spy satellite. They witnessed the fighter jets falling, knew that the Russian strategic military bases had been inactive for over 12 hours after that incident, and had images of the enormous UFO that had appeared over the Volga, with a diameter of over two miles. This is why the U.S. military had learned their lesson and refrained from making any hostile moves against the craft that appeared in front of the United Nations building. They only sent a couple of drones, initially joined by a police drone and three helicopters from TV networks. However, with each passing minute, the number of news and police helicopters grew. They all resembled a swarm of small insects circling the colossal black craft.

The sight of that immense UFO just a few hundred yards away, with helicopters buzzing around it, made it impossible to think about anything else. The atmosphere in the room was highly charged. The security service arrived, intending to evacuate us from the building, but the Secretary-General, in her first act of courage, refused. Instead, we moved the meeting to her office, which also had a view of the UFO. Within minutes, the room filled with heads of departments, advisors, and high-ranking UN officials. Everyone was baffled by such an unbelievable and unexpected situation. Some suffered panic attacks and had to leave the room, while Elisa remained calm.

"It's urgent to convene the General Assembly..." Elisa said, looking at the Secretary-General.

At that moment, the UN Secretary-General realized she could no longer deny the situation. She turned to her Chief of Staff and asked about the shortest possible time to hold such a meeting. The Chief of Staff, captivated by the spectacle outside the window, took several seconds to respond.

"From a legal perspective, considering the chamber's regulations..." she began.

"I don't care about the regulations," the Secretary-General interrupted. "I just need to know how long it will take to notify the governments of all countries and all media outlets to attend a virtual meeting."

She continued, "I also need to know how much time it will take to have the information technology infrastructure ready for the meeting and for it to be broadcasted online worldwide. We have to notify the translation team and all personnel not to leave their offices in half an hour when the workday ends. Please, for a moment, forget about what you're seeing and get everything activated."

It appeared the Secretary-General had recovered from the shock. Twenty minutes later, the Chief of Staff returned to announce that the virtual meeting could be held within three hours, and it was scheduled for that time. Elisa requested accommodations to prepare and rest, and then she left. With a glance, she told me we would talk later. The rest of us remained in the room, waiting, hypnotized by the images visible through the window.

Television stations worldwide broadcasted images of the colossal UFO. On one channel, the anchor recounted Elisa's journey since the Moscow attack, her liberation 40 days later, and her presence at the United Nations headquarters in New York, where she was currently in a meeting with the Secretary-General. They also informed the audience that an extraordinary General Assembly would take place in a few hours, broadcasted globally via the internet and television, during which Elisa had a message for all of humanity from the alien civilization that had rescued her. Initial estimates suggested that 85 percent of humanity would tune in, an unprecedented level of global viewership. A phenomenon was occurring in the planet's night zones, with neighbors waking each other up to ensure no one missed the message. The Earth stayed awake for the next few hours.

XXIII

The Message

From the moment the Secretary-General of the United Nations decided to convene the virtual General Assembly, she did everything in her power to assist Elisa in achieving her goal. She ordered that Elisa's address be delivered from the podium with the backdrop of green-veined marble, the same podium from which heads of state address the assembly. No one else but Elisa would use that podium, giving her intervention the highest institutional relevance. After being introduced by the Secretary-General as the person bearing a message from an alien civilization to humanity, she was given the floor.

Elisa began her address by thanking the Secretary-General of the UN for convening the assembly and all the world leaders for their attendance. "But above all," she said, "I am grateful to the billions of citizens of this planet who are listening to me now, because it is for you that the alien civilization is sending this message.

"The extraterrestrial life I have encountered is so advanced and so different from ours that it is barely comprehensible. Their technology can accomplish what seems impossible.

"For 40 days, I have had to answer many questions; my psyche, and with it, the human mind, has been analyzed. I have also been shown different ways of thinking and approaching reality. The alien civilization that has welcomed me is considering whether to protect us from the Plague, and it has not made a decision yet. In that decision, creativity is in our favor, while violence and cynicism are against us.

"The civilization that has saved my life is a collective mind of over a trillion beings from various species. One of their principles is not to interfere with the natural flow of events in the universe, except in highly justified cases. Their decision to defend us from the Plague must be one of those highly justified cases, and it depends on what we, as humans, do from now on.

"Despite our societies being dominated by the most primitive beings, obsessed with personal success and reaching the top, the alien civilization recognizes that we have begun to change our model and become increasingly respectful of other living beings and nature. But it knows that what is happening in Europe is not enough, and there is no certainty that this movement will ultimately succeed. It is more likely that the changes we have initiated will dissolve, and we will continue to exploit each other and deplete the planet in the same way the Plague does.

"Eliminating hunger and destitution worldwide will lead to a society where it will be easier for us to start treating each other with respect. Ending the confinement of animals in terrible conditions will help us overcome part of human brutality, not killing other beings for food will provide us with honor. To solve the situation, we must ensure that well-being is accessible to all the inhabitants of Earth; we must be capable of providing renewable energy, 3D printers, food incubators, and access to raw materials for everyone. It is the well-off countries that must facilitate this, so I propose that this be the first issue we address in the collective intelligence network, among the inhabitants of countries that can meet these needs for the rest of the world.

"But all of the above will not be enough. Society is an external projection of the psychological states of all its members. We have created this society, and we generate order or confusion with our way of life. There will be no significant change until each individual changes. If we can transform ourselves, give a different focus to our daily existence, we will influence the world as a whole. It is necessary to build a new structure on new foundations, on new facts and values. This is the responsibility of each one of us; we have to rediscover values and build on deeper and more solid foundations.

"We must be aware that we are all traveling on the same ship, our planet, and we share the same fate. We must realize the importance of building a better and fairer world, of behaving honorably and civilized towards each other and with all other living beings, of adopting a respectful attitude toward nature, of harnessing synergies and focusing on relevant matters. In essence, of behaving intelligently and not allowing destruction to be a part of our way of life.

"I believe that a majority expects something like this to happen. For that to occur, it is also essential that the internet is accessible to the inhabitants of the Earth and that everyone can participate in collective intelligence. This will enhance our creativity as a species and bolster the self-esteem of each individual, along with their identification with common projects. This flourishing will allow us to embark on a new heroic era of the intellect and stop generating chaos, unhappiness, destruction, fear, and cruelty. Perhaps this way, we can think about being protected from the Plague's invasion.

"But we must act quickly, as we do not have much time. We have ten years to do so before the Plague arrives with the intention of exterminating us."

After her address, debates commenced during which leaders of various governments requested the floor. However, the Secretary-General of the UN was no longer focused on that. She approached Elisa to express her gratitude for choosing the UN to deliver her message, wish her the best of luck, assure her of their support, and offer assistance in any way they could. She also informed us that the enormous cylindrical spacecraft had disappeared the moment Elisa began to speak.

Elisa requested two tickets on the first flight departing for Europe, and the Secretary-General offered the organization's jet for the journey, along with diplomatic immunity. 45 minutes later, we were taking off from John F. Kennedy Airport.

XXIV

The Transformation

Since we had last seen each other at the UN, I had wanted to tell Elisa what had happened to me, although I was more interested in hearing about her. But it was impossible to exchange a word; now, on the plane, the moment had finally come.

"How are you feeling, Elisa?" I inquired.

"Exhausted. And worried about what needs to be set in motion."

"Take a moment to relax. Breathe deeply and don't think about anything."

Not even 20 seconds had passed before she began to speak.

"I watched the footage of my rescue in Moscow in a recording, and I was surprised by how quickly the UFO that saved my life ascended because that acceleration should have crushed me to the ground. But I didn't feel a thing. At first, I thought I hadn't even moved from the spot."

"They calculated that the acceleration at which the spacecraft took off was over 300 'g,' and nothing can survive that. I was very concerned." -I said.

"I also saw that the missile explosion was huge, causing hundreds of casualties and completely destroying the entire square." Elisa continued, "I didn't notice anything—no noise, no trembling. But, for some reason, what surprised me the most is that the object that picked me up looked so small on the outside, but on the inside, it was much larger, with an almost organic appearance and a shape that changed progressively and almost constantly. I remained there for 40 days, although it felt like only one. During that time, I didn't get to see any aliens; all my contact with them was mental. I learned new ways of thinking."

"New ways of thinking, I heard you mention that in your speech at the UN."

"The first thing I had to learn during those 40 days," Elisa continued, "was that understanding is now, not tomorrow; tomorrow is for the lazy mind. Putting things off until tomorrow is pointless because perception only occurs in the present. Transformation can only happen instantly, in the now. To access understanding, you need to understand yourself, observe how your own thought processes work, and that requires being very attentive, not identifying with anything, comparing, or judging. You need to start by adopting a passive attitude, focused on contemplation, to realize the reasons behind each of our actions. This way, the profound content of our thought, its meaning, becomes visible."

Elisa was unrecognizable. She seemed cold and distant, but at the same time, her body expressed total trust in me. We had hugged when we first saw each other in New York, and we hadn't touched since. She appeared rigid, and I thought she was trying to control the shock of having undergone a 40-day abduction. She seemed exhausted, yet also possessed by the excitement of her discoveries. She continued speaking.

"When you focus on contemplation, you understand not only the surface layers of consciousness but also the deeper ones—where our motives and intentions, demands, anxieties, urgencies, and fears reside. It's where our thoughts boil and come into contact with those of others. It's where you can contemplate the impulses that move others, with any conversation partner you encounter. To do that, you need to be aware from moment to moment of your thoughts and feelings, not just when you are awake, but also when you project all sorts of symbols onto consciousness that we interpret as dreams. This way, you reach a state in which the self is absent, and you open the door to the hidden, to what is real and immeasurable."

At that moment, I realized that of everything happening, the change that had occurred in Elisa was what mattered to me the most.

"You're different," I affirmed.

"I've achieved a symbiosis with the alien that abducted us," she said. "Now, it sees through my eyes and hears through my ears. You and I are three."

XXV

New Relationship

It wasn't easy to adapt to the new situation. My deep admiration for Elisa remained intact, for her courage and intelligence, her perseverance, her ability to understand and empathize with others, her originality and independence, and her idealism that drove every one of her actions. But from the very beginning, I realized that our intimate relationship couldn't continue in the current circumstances. It was hard to behave naturally around her. I couldn't ignore the fact that a third party was always present. I believed she felt the same way. The coldness and distance that I had noticed in her since we first met in New York, which contrasted with her usual spontaneity, had to have a reason, and part of it was likely related to this.

However, she underwent a catharsis that allowed her to see reality from a different perspective. She referred to it as a new way of thinking that led to essential and profound changes. To explain it to me, she mentioned 'Dark Matter' a novel she had read a few years ago. The novel described the development of a civilization on a distant planet where beings used echolocation instead of sight. Similar to bats, they emitted high-pitched sounds that bounced off objects and returned to their ears, allowing them to perceive their surroundings, such as determining if an animal's fur was soft or rough, if a rock was damp, if a surface was hard or soft, or if a fabric was porous or impermeable. With this sense, they perceived their environment more accurately than humans with sight, as if they had a form of remote touch. These beings had developed an advanced society with remarkable science and technology. Since sound waves required an atmosphere to propagate, however, they could not detect the vast expanse of stars or the two moons orbiting their planet when looking at the sky. As a result, they believed that their Earth-like planet represented the entire universe.

Elisa explained that, like them, we live in a virtual world created by our minds based on the information received from our limited senses, which do not perceive much of reality. Now, she was starting to expand that horizon, realizing that many of our beliefs are based on our limited perception of the environment.

During our trip to Paris, I shared my experience aboard the Plague's ship the fourth time I entered the flow. It was intimidating because I knew that a third party was also listening, but I was willing to do anything to maintain trust in our relationship.

I asked Elisa why the UFO had dropped her off in Moscow instead of directly at the UN headquarters.

Elisa told me that the alien who had saved her life in Moscow, the same one who had abducted us ten years ago, her now permanent intimate companion, had very detailed information about any human. He knew that the Russian president had planned to revive his heroic image within the country (which had deteriorated considerably over the last decade). To achieve this, the president intended to "teach a lesson" to the alien invaders about the inviolability of Russian territory. He also hoped to bolster patriotism among the inhabitants of the "largest country on the planet" and earn the respect of other major military powers. The president, an elderly psychopath, had little to lose, as his life expectancy was short. It was worth taking the risk, even if the initiative failed and put the entire planet in jeopardy.

Elisa's intimate companion wanted humanity, especially Russia, to understand their level of technology and thus prevent future aggression attempts. That's why she had to speak to the Russian president so that he could see firsthand that he was dealing with a vastly superior technology in every aspect, against which he could do nothing.

"You took a great risk." - I said.

"No, I could be rescued at any moment, just as I was in the Plaza of the Space Conquerors."

"I suppose" - I said - "the UFO's appearance when the UN Secretary-General opposed the assembly's convocation was not a coincidence either."

"It wasn't, but I was also surprised by the way my permanent intimate companion helped us."

XXVI

Preparations

Two weeks after Elisa's speech at the UN, we were summoned by the Secretary-General to a meeting of an expert committee consisting of individuals from various fields of science and politics at the organization's headquarters in Geneva. Elisa apologized for her absence.

We gathered beneath the vast dome of the General Assembly Hall. The ceiling had been decorated decades ago to resemble the surface of a colorful extraterrestrial planet, which its creator defined as a cave-planet that unites people and travels to the future. It struck me as an appropriate setting for the topics we were about to discuss. There were more than 600 people in attendance, and the Secretary-General presided over the meeting. The entire event was broadcast via cable in real-time (it had been recently prohibited worldwide to transmit information using electromagnetic waves that could escape into outer space).

Over the course of eight days, we deliberated on various topics related to the Plague: what kind of technology they might possess, how we could neutralize it, how to organize the defense of the planet, which global agreements should be adopted, how to secure assistance from the civilization that had saved Elisa from the assassination attempt, and how to detect Plague ships as early as possible when they were still far from our planet. The latter was the first issue we addressed.

After a lengthy discussion, Robert Weryk, the astronomer who discovered 'Oumuamua, the interstellar object that passed through the solar system in 2017, spoke up:

"Seventeen years ago, our Pan-STARRS telescope allowed us to detect 'Oumuamua when it was 0.2 astronomical units from Earth, which is a distance of 20 million miles. It came from the star Vega in the Lyra constellation. If it were a dark object, it would be roughly 600 feet in size, and if its surface was bright, less than half of that. It appeared as a small streak in the sky and was at the limits of what the telescope could detect."

"If my data is correct," the Secretary-General remarked, "that distance is quite short. Mars is 40 million miles away. If we can only detect invaders when they have already passed Mars and are halfway to Earth, we won't have time to react."

Anne-Marie Lagrange, the director of the VLT (Very Large Telescope), which, at 72 years old, remained full of vitality, then took the floor.

"Our telescope is more powerful than the one used to detect 'Oumuamua. With it, we photographed a giant exoplanet for the first time. However, it is still not enough to detect Plague ships, that will be at most a few thousand meters in size, before they reach Mars. However, there is an advantage in our optical system: it allows for easy scaling of the mirror's size to make it enormous. It's just a matter of money."

"I suppose a telescope's power lies in the size of its mirror, enabling it to see further and more precisely," said the Secretary-General.

"Exactly," replied Didier Queloz, the discoverer of the first extrasolar planet. "We don't have any telescopes with the capacity to detect Plague ships beyond the distance of Mars. Even with our most powerful telescopes, such as the Extremely Large Telescope with its 40-meter mirror. Not even the James Webb Space Telescope can do the job. But I agree that if we combine our expertise in constructing massive mirrors with the interferometry technology of Lagrange's VLT, we can achieve observations equivalent to what could be done with a mirror a couple of kilometers in diameter."

"It sounds like very good news, especially if you could clarify what you mean by interferometry," the Secretary-General said, annoyed by the technical jargon.

"Interferometry," Queloz continued, "allows us to combine the light received by dozens of telescopes that work simultaneously and in coordination in a single image. It involves treating light as a wave, not a photon, and working with its interference pattern. This way, we can obtain a highly detailed image. If we distribute individual telescopes with 50-meter mirrors in a circle two or three kilometers in diameter and use interferometry to coordinate the light received by each of them, we can detect the Plague when it exits the Oort Cloud, a light-year away."

"How much would it cost?" the Secretary-General asked.

"Approximately ten billion."

"With that sum, could it be done in a couple of years?" the Secretary-General asked again.

"In such a short timeframe, it would be fifteen billion. Additionally, we would need two telescopes, one in each hemisphere, to cover the entire celestial vault, as we don't know where the Plague will come from. Thirty billion."

The expert committee was established on a permanent basis, and its members would remain in continuous contact. The Secretary-General of the UN committed to submitting all initiatives arising from the meeting to collective intelligence before presenting them to the General Assembly. It was an acknowledgment at the highest level of something that was already evident to many: the immense creativity of collective intelligence.

XXVII

With Elisa

Since Elisa's speech before the UN, she disappeared from public life; she didn't participate in conferences, meetings, or events, didn't grant interviews, issue press releases, or engage in the collective intelligence web. I was the only person she maintained contact with and, in a way, played the role of her unofficial spokesperson – though with little success as all kinds of rumors started circulating about her, tarnishing her reputation. Worse for me, since she had been returned to the Conquerors of Space square, she became increasingly distant and elusive, far from the person I had known. Up until then, Elisa and I had been lovers, but it became impossible to rekindle an intimate relationship after her return, and the closeness we once shared was severed by an invisible barrier.

Although she had secluded herself in her home, I was reluctant to stop seeing her, and on occasion, I visited her. During those visits, Elisa always made me feel welcomed and loved; however, I couldn't avoid experiencing inner lament for the distance between us, a feeling of pain that also saddened her.

Less than two months had passed since her liberation in Moscow when one afternoon, she told me that her mind was now much broader, and through her intimate relationship with her permanent companion, she had discovered other realities that had changed her.

"I've tried to push my thoughts as far as I could," she said. "I've remained silent, perceptive, I've observed without comparing, detached from my own existence, as if I were someone else. Instead of judging, I've wanted to understand, I've observed, and that's how I began to comprehend the being with whom I'm in constant contact. I share their thoughts, and that's also a form of love."

Upon hearing these words, I was overcome by the sensation of having lost Elisa.

"I have fundamentally changed," she continued. "To come to understand the new reality I live in, I needed to detach myself from my ego, to look from a distance, and do so continuously. I seek to comprehend the immeasurable, and I can only achieve it if my mind operates without any belief patterns, if my thinking no longer responds to sensations triggered by the senses, if I observe the new without relying on previous knowledge, and if I reflect without directing my experiences, ambitions, pursuits, and desires."

I thanked Elisa for her honesty while simultaneously suffering from not being able to play any role in her new existence. I belonged to the experiences, ambitions, pursuits, and desires that Elisa had to exclude from her thoughts. I felt like a relic from the past, valuable sentimentally but lacking in functionality. I didn't doubt that Elisa still loved me, but her love for me had become small compared to the new horizons she now glimpsed.

"When I achieve complete self-forgetfulness, I reach a state where there is no effort or struggle, only a feeling of peace. At that moment, I manage to understand my intimate companion and discover love. Where there is love, there is no self."

Elisa immersed herself in a world of introspection that demanded sincerity and clarity of thought, with no other occupation or commitment that would hinder her reflection. For her, only the present existed, and her life unfolded within that reality. Her silence and withdrawal from public life, at such a crucial moment for humanity, remained inexplicable to most and produced deep shock in everyone.

I felt desolate. Perhaps I hadn't entirely lost Elisa, but now she was very distant.

XXVIII

Renaissance

When Elisa spoke at the UN, it had been nine years since a political party that embraced direct governance by the citizens had won the elections in France. Three years after that, they established a system of liquid democracy in their parliament, the National Assembly. This system allowed the citizens to directly and individually participate in the National Assembly's votes, and when they did so, the representatives lost some of their representational power. If half of the electorate voted on an issue, each parliamentarian's representational capacity was reduced by half. The result of the vote in the Assembly on any topic was a simple sum of the direct votes of the citizens and those contributed by the parliamentarians, based on their current level of representativeness.

These advancements in democracy led to significant decisions that transformed society. Optimism, faith in the future, fascination with making the world a different and better place, the desire to be part of this movement, and the honor of belonging to it spread widely. A renaissance occurred, as people reevaluated their personal goals, work, health, money, and spiritual beliefs. Profound changes in thought took place, heralding a new beginning with more realistic ideals. Accumulating, consuming, and living a material-driven life became outdated. Power, money, and possessions as a means of marking an individual's importance were replaced by other values. Nothing was more important than personal commitment or a promise given. Pleasant interactions and culture were appreciated. Altruism, solidarity, social entrepreneurship, courage, and honesty became qualities that made people attractive. Generosity toward the community garnered immense popularity, and equality, the absence of hierarchies in treatment despite economic differences or public responsibilities, became an unquestioned social value. Flaunting power or wealth was considered distasteful, and abuses of power were unforgivable. Nationalism, patriotism, paranoid views of others, and religious radicalism all faded away.

The National Assembly passed the Essential Basic Goods Act, which guaranteed the supply of essential goods to all citizens: housing, food incubators, 3D printers, access to the internet, and enough renewable energy to meet their needs. The basic income had already been approved before this. The law stipulated that the production of 3D printers and food incubators had to be automated and nationalized. In a short time, both products were manufactured automatically with the involvement of robots and artificial intelligence. Raw materials entered one end of the factory, and at the other end, 3D printers or food incubators emerged without human intervention. This technology was made available to any country that requested it.

All of this occurred over a period of nine years. The enthusiasm with which everyone embarked on the project exceeded all expectations. While humanity had seen profound changes in a short time before, this was perhaps the most spectacular. During these nine years, whenever elections were held in a country, especially in Europe, the party whose electoral program adhered to what had been agreed upon in the web of collective participation typically won. The European Union was reconstituted by a large group of countries that decided to abolish the right of veto and imposed fiscal, labor, health, educational, and welfare harmonization. This new European Union spoke with a single voice in foreign policy.

The model established in France was a dazzling beacon that everyone wanted to approach, and the citizens had an increasing say in global affairs.

It was then that Elisa and I recorded the video explaining that we had been abducted and warned of the impending Plague. This video caused a lot of confusion and doubts about our credibility. However, shortly afterward, when Elisa was saved from the assassination attempt and then returned to deliver a message from an alien civilization at the UN, very few doubted that the Plague threat was real. Knowing that there was something that could be done to prevent our extermination prevented the demoralization of many people who wanted to contribute wholeheartedly to Elisa's proposed project, viewing it as salvation.

Two months had passed since Elisa's speech at the UN when her initiative to provide Essential Basic Goods to anyone in need worldwide was put into action. It was an agreement of the United Nations General Assembly that created a coalition formed by Australia, Canada, Chile, China, the European Union, Japan, New Zealand, South Korea, Tunisia, Uruguay and the USA. Some of these countries were responsible for setting up automated factories for 3D printers and food incubators where they were needed, while other coalition members installed automated renewable energy generator factories. Governments receiving aid were required to guarantee public education and healthcare and provide the necessary raw materials to build the factories and meet the basic needs of their citizens. Automated agricultural and mining production systems were installed. A vast number of volunteers wanted to participate in the project and worked efficiently and swiftly.

Six years had passed since Elisa's speech at the UN when the basic needs of hundreds of millions of people were beginning to be met in places that had previously known only hunger and poverty. It was an achievement of idealism and solidarity like never before.

XXIX

Security Council

The UN Security Council has five permanent members with veto power (China, USA, France, UK, and Russia), as well as ten temporary members elected every two years as regional representatives without veto power. The Security Council, whose decisions are binding on the rest of the world's nations, can authorize the use of force if the agreement is supported by nine of its members, unless one of the five permanent member countries exercises its veto power.

Two weeks after the meeting of experts at the UN headquarters in Geneva, there was a meeting of the UN Security Council in which the three superpowers of the planet, China, the USA, and Russia, proposed allocating a significant portion of Earth's resources for military preparations to repel the invasion of the Plague. France subjected its vote on this initiative to the decision of its citizens on the collective participation platform.

The debates among the French were intense. In the end, the largest group on the platform believed that relying on the opinion that an alien civilization might have of humanity was very risky and too uncertain when it came to the survival of the species. Another group conditioned its support for the proposal on the guarantee that it would not affect the commitment to providing well-being to the entire population of the planet. This latter position was ultimately accepted by all members of the UN Security Council, agreeing to unite the military efforts of all countries to defend Earth.

The defense plan focused on a project developed over the past 17 years to send small ships to the planets of the Alpha Centauri star, as recommended by the committee of experts two weeks earlier at the Geneva meeting. The Starshot Breakthrough Initiative was conceived by cosmologists Avi Loeb and Philip Lubin in 2015, endorsed by Stephen Hawking, and funded in 2019 by the Russian technology billionaire Yuri Milner. To carry it out, a massive array of lasers was built in the Atacama Desert, operating in synchrony to create a single beam of light with 100 gigawatts of power. This immense energy condensed into a beam of light was designed to launch tiny spacecraft at a speed of 37,000 miles per second, enabling them to reach the Alpha Centauri star in just 20 years.

The project became more complex due to difficulties in miniaturizing the instruments of interstellar spacecraft, leading to the installation of new lasers to increase power to 1000 gigawatts. With this immense power, a thousand small probes were successfully launched toward Alpha Centauri at a speed of 37,000 miles per second. Once this goal was achieved, the Starshot laser system was used to send a crewed spacecraft to Mars on a journey of just 28 days, propelled by a sail that collected the laser beam.

The UN Security Council, which approved the union of efforts for Earth's defense, considered the Starshot project an extremely valuable resource to face the challenge ahead.

XXX

Sighting

On Christmas Day of 2044, it had been 10 years, 5 months, and 17 days since Elisa's speech at the UN when the interferometry telescope in the northern hemisphere, with a resolution equivalent to a 1.8-mile diameter mirror, detected a bright spot in the infrared range with an estimated temperature of about 15,000 degrees Celsius, at a distance of almost one light-year. Another interferometry telescope installed on the far side of the Moon, through triangulation, detected the movement of the light spot. It was moving towards Earth at a speed of approximately 1,700 miles per second, accelerating at 2.3 "g."

The object was approaching Earth from the north, outside the plane where all the planets orbit, and its point of origin was pointing towards the star Vega, only 25 light-years from Earth. At that moment, everyone remembered that Oumuamua had also come from the same direction, 27 years earlier.

The data obtained from the object, especially the high temperature observed, matched some of the scientific predictions made in the UN expert committee meeting held in Geneva 10 years prior. During that meeting, scientists agreed that if the Plague's ships could travel at nearly the speed of light, they would need some kind of force shield to protect them from constant micrometeoroid impacts. There is no area in space within our part of the galaxy, known as the Local Bubble, that is not filled with this "space dust" dispersed by a supernova explosion four million years ago. These micrometeoroids range in size from a speck of dust to a tennis ball. The density of this "space dust" is such that if a medium-sized spacecraft were to travel in a straight line through space, it would collide with one of these particles every 7,000 miles. This may not seem like much, but at speeds approaching the speed of light, there would be dozens of high-energy impacts every second, enough to destroy any object that did not use some form of force shield (a physical shield appeared to be a less likely alternative because it would need to be several miles thick to survive a journey of just a few light-years).

In the debate held in Geneva ten years earlier, the director of the ITER project explained that their organization had created fusion energy, the same as stars produce, by stably confining hydrogen plasma within a magnetic field at 12,000 degrees Celsius.

"That temperature is twice that of the Sun's surface," he said, "and it would vaporize any micrometeoroids that collide with the plasma, as long as their size does not exceed a few inches in diameter, as is assumed to be the case with space dust. For now, we have only been able to confine plasma within a toroidal cylinder, inside a large hollow donut. Although we lack the technology to maintain plasma confinement in the form of a large screen, in theory, this is possible if we create a magnetic field that contains it in three dimensions."

It was ruled out that the entire ship could be covered by a plasma shield because it would be inside an oven with tens of thousands of degrees, where nothing could survive without vaporizing. Instead, it was considered that the plasma shield would be installed at a certain distance at the front of the ship, which would be sufficient to fulfill its purpose.

Therefore, it was highly likely that what we had detected on Christmas Day in 2044 was not the Star of Bethlehem but the first glimpse of the plasma shield of a Plague ship heading towards our planet with the intention of annihilating us. It was at a distance of almost one light-year, and what we were seeing had occurred a year ago. Based on our knowledge of their method of navigation (as explained by the alien who abducted Elisa and me), we calculated that the ship would need just under two years to reach Earth. Subtracting the year that had passed since the images were captured at that moment, we had about 10 months before the Plague reached our planet.

XXXI

Fear

On October 30, 1938, Orson Welles broadcasted "The War of the Worlds" on the radio, a 59-minute fake news program that 1.7 million listeners believed to be true, creating mass hysteria. According to a study by psychologist Hadley Cantril, never before had so many people been suddenly and intensely shaken, with streets and public spaces in every locality across the country filled with people in distress. On that occasion, the station clarified after the program that it was a prank to celebrate Halloween. But on Christmas Day in 2044, there would be no such retraction.

Knowing that the Plague had already passed the Oort Cloud and was heading towards Earth at an increasingly faster speed of thousands of miles per second, panic spread across the planet. Houses of worship from all religions were packed with believers. There were mass suicides, some driven by cults that preyed on the most vulnerable minds. There was also a movement called "The Resistance," whose members built a network of interconnected underground bunkers stocked with water, weapons, raw materials for 3D printers, and repositories of stem cells for food incubators. These behaviors were reminiscent of what had occurred during the Cold War, but this time they were much more extreme.

Nothing provides greater relief than being able to blame someone else for your misfortunes. Many fanatic groups sought to blame Elisa and me for everything that was happening. They did not forgive Elisa for disappearing from public life, for not even revealing where she lived, and they speculated about the possibility that she had left for the planet of the alien civilization that had saved her life. I didn't know her whereabouts either. We were both blamed for not doing more to get that civilization to intervene on our behalf and save us from the Plague.

But despite all this, in general terms, humanity had changed for the better in recent years. There was greater respect for nature in all its forms, and thanks to the guaranteed coverage of basic needs and collective intelligence, our level of civilization, honorability, and rationality had increased. The latter had led to an exponential growth of creativity in the collective intelligence web.

A few years before the Plague became visible in the outer reaches of the solar system, a defense strategy had been developed on the collective intelligence web. Its first measure was that the first attack should not be launched against the Plague without ensuring its lethality. Essentially, this meant destroying them in the first blow to prevent their counterattack. This implied that if we were to initiate hostilities with our Starshot lasers, we had to wait until the invaders were two and a half million miles away, as their immense power diminished with distance and lost its destructive force beyond that range. To most of us, postponing the first attack until the enemy was so close, only five times farther away than the Moon, seemed too risky, and we needed to explore other alternatives.

We could attack the Plague when they were farther away if, instead of using direct laser shots, we launched atomic bombs. In this strategy, we would use the Starshot lasers to send our most powerful hydrogen bombs with solar sails. It was considered that we could intercept the invading ships when they were 24 light minutes away from Earth, at 280 million miles. Our bombs could reach them in six months, propelled by the Starshot lasers, and the Plague's ships would have slowed down sufficiently, after 97 days of deceleration, for us to intercept them. However, this strategy had a significant flaw: if we used the lasers to send bombs against the invaders, the Plague could detect their location and destroy our Starshot facilities in a counterattack, thereby nullifying the most valuable weapons in our defense.

For this reason, it was considered preferable to launch these bombs using conventional rockets. As this propulsion system is much slower than solar sails propelled by the Starshot lasers, we could only intercept the Plague at a much closer distance, four light minutes away, at 47 million miles from Earth. The fact that this was the only viable alternative for our first line of defense did not sit well with almost anyone because it meant that, at that moment, the Plague would have only 27 days left to reach our planet. Everyone wondered whether it was really the case that we had to wait for the invading ships to be so close before we could begin defending ourselves.

No one came up with a better option, however, and now that we had just detected the bright point signaling the arrival of the invaders to our solar system, it was almost time to launch those missiles that would take 244 days to cover 47 million miles to intercept the Plague. The difference in technology between them and us was striking, considering that at the maximum speed achieved by the Plague on its journey, it had taken just over four minutes to cover distances for which we needed more than eight months.

I suppose reflections like these had pushed many people to fervently hope that the Plague was not what it seemed but rather a peaceful civilization. They considered that Elisa and I might have been deceived by their enemies to trick humanity into attacking them and prevent the possibility of forming an alliance. The idea began to spread that the best way to approach the situation was to send a message of peace. I understood the appeal of this idea, and I would have liked to believe it too, that everything had been a false alarm caused by two easily suggestible idiots. Unfortunately, I knew all too well that the Plague was a real and terrible threat.

Nonetheless, the idea that the Plague could be a peaceful civilization and that Elisa and I had been deceived was so enticing that it spread quickly. It bolstered a movement that believed it was necessary to attempt contact with the Plague before launching an attack. Essentially, their message was:

"We cannot simply attack the first civilization approaching from the outer reaches of the solar system. We must seek an alliance, and if that is not possible, we should ask them to leave before initiating an attack. We cannot start a war with an extraterrestrial civilization that is approaching us, of which we know very little; we cannot take such a momentous step solely based on the accounts of two people."

This message was overwhelmingly popular in the debates. Three weeks passed, and we saw how the bright light detected by our telescopes broke up into five smaller points. It was a fleet that was approaching us.

XXXII

The Confession

The moment was approaching when the missiles, which would take 244 days to intercept the Plague, had to be launched, and the pacifist movement had gained such strength that it had almost reached the majority.

For years, I had concealed that I had seen the Plague, that I had been inside their ship, that I know what they are like and their intentions. I had never found the right time to tell it; such a narrative, even in times as open-minded as the ones we were living, seemed too unbelievable, and I had no proof of what had happened to me. But despite everything, the time had come to tell the story.

I told everything, and I did it for everyone to hear; it was one of the most-watched recordings on the internet in many years. I explained my first experience in the linden garden and the feeling of entering the flow; I recounted the kidnapping and liberation of a brave woman; I spoke about the quantum being, the reality in which it lives, my telepathic communication with it, how incomprehensible its existence in 10 dimensions is to us, how it transported my mind to a Plague ship, and what I experienced there. It was a story for which I had no evidence; I knew that many people would think I was completely crazy, which is why I had kept silent until then.

Indeed, many thought I was crazy, others a charlatan, and they all hurled the worst insults and threats at me. But my detailed information about what the enemy was like was the only one available; many speculations had been made, but none had provided such a concrete image of the Plague insects and their intentions. These descriptions became part of the collective imagination almost instantly and had an unconscious effect on the majority. In the end, the fear that what I was recounting might be true and that we might be defenseless against such terrible beings had enough weight in our decision, and the proposal formulated by the collective intelligence before the United Nations General Assembly was to launch the first missile attack against the Plague.

XXXIII

Preliminaries

Since we first detected the five Plague ships, they had continued to increase their speed in the direction of Earth. As they accelerated, the white light they emitted initially began to shift toward blue and then into the ultraviolet range. This light, which our eyes couldn't perceive, could only be shown to us by the sensors of our telescopes. The invading ships must have been traveling at nearly the speed of light.

It was impossible not to be awed by the spectacle and the incredible amount of energy required to propel these enormous ships at such speeds. Most scientists believed that this colossal propulsion involved harnessing the energy produced when antimatter particles collided with matter. They assumed the Plague must have particle accelerators of immense power on board, enabling them to create antimatter. However, some physicists believed this immense energy could also originate from hyperforce, the fifth fundamental force of nature that had been detected starting from muons at Fermilab a quarter of a century earlier and was thought to be the source of dark energy, a repulsive force of such magnitude that pushes galaxies apart.

When the distance between the invaders and us had been reduced to 21 light-days, the ships began the deceleration process that would allow them to reach our planet at a much slower speed and enter Earth's orbit. We had imagined that for this maneuver, they would need to disable their plasma shields and rotate the ship 180 degrees so that their thrusters would be pointed toward our world to initiate deceleration. From that point onward, they still had 150 days of continuous deceleration at 2.3 "g."

This was the moment when we could finally see the five ships, which had been hidden behind their bright plasma shields until then. They had an organic, pod-like shape with no straight lines or perfect curves, just a somewhat rough surface. During this 180-degree turn, we had a detailed view of their exterior appearance and calculated their size to be roughly three miles in length by one in diameter, although none of them were exactly the same as the others.

Before they had completed the turning maneuver, one of the ships exploded in a massive flash. We thought that at that critical moment, when the ships were not protected by their plasma shields, they might have been hit by a meteorite. Not only were we relieved by the disappearance of an enemy ship, but the brilliance of its explosion also revealed some small points accompanying the motherships, resembling an swarm. They had an organic shape similar to the motherships but were much smaller and elongated, about 200 feet in length and only 30 in diameter. These capsules did not initiate the braking process and continued their journey to Earth at nearly 186,000 miles per second. At that speed, they would reach Earth in 21 days, long before our hydrogen bomb missiles could intercept the invading fleet.

Even though they did not use propulsion (they were traveling by inertia), it was not difficult to identify and track the trajectory of this swarm of ships approaching Earth at nearly the speed of light. There were 13 of them. Given their speed, attempting to hit objects traveling 186,000 miles in a single second with missiles was impossible. They could only be intercepted by Starshot's lasers. Although the power of our lasers was substantial, it was limited. To ensure successful shots, we had to wait until the enemy ships were less than 1.2 million miles away, seven seconds before they could reach Earth at their current speed. Fortunately, the ships maintained a straight trajectory, so we knew where they would be when they were within firing range, and it was just a matter of aiming at that point and activating the lasers when the ships passed through it. The three Starshot installations in the northern hemisphere had only one second to destroy the first three enemy ships before targeting and firing on the next three in the following second, and so on until all 13 invading vessels were destroyed in those seven seconds.

For 20 days, we conducted simulations of this firing cadence, and even though we achieved significant coordination, no one was sure if the strategy would actually work.

What added to our anxiety was the fact that we would have to reveal the location of our laser facilities to the Plague in the preliminary stages of the battle, making them vulnerable when we couldn't yet fire at their motherships. There was no alternative, however, to preventing this swarm of ships from impacting Earth. The immense energy that would be produced if even one of these ships collided with our planet at nearly the speed of light was deeply troubling. Everyone recalled that the energy released by these objects would be half of the result of multiplying their mass by their velocity squared, almost equivalent to the explosion of a gigantic atomic bomb.

Twenty-one days passed while humanity held its breath. There was immense anxiety and nervousness. We felt some relief when, during their journey, three of the thirteen Plague's ships were destroyed, possibly due to collisions with meteorites.

With just minutes left to fire the lasers, the remaining ten ships ignited their retrothrusters and began to decelerate with an enormous force of 700 "g." Adjustments had to be made to the lasers because the arrival time at the firing point varied, and their trajectory underwent minor alterations during the deceleration process. Nothing resembled what we had been rehearsing. Fortunately, these missiles with their brilliant retrothrusters were easy to track, and Starshot's precision aiming was one of its best qualities.

Nevertheless, the first shots missed a target still moving at high speeds, with different velocities and trajectories than anticipated. We had to wait for some time until the three laser facilities in the northern hemisphere could make the necessary corrections for the second volley. In this instance, we destroyed two of the missiles, which exploded in a massive blast.

All of this was being broadcast live, and the shouts of joy when those two missiles were destroyed could be heard all over the planet.

Only eight remained now, and we had even less time to shoot them down as they were at a shorter distance and moving more slowly.

In the third volley, we destroyed three more missiles. Only five were left. The fourth salvo neutralized another three, and there was no time for another shot. The remaining two missiles entered Earth's atmosphere in a vertical position and at a very wide angle, with some navigation system keeping them in that position and preventing them from bouncing off the atmosphere. The air resistance slowed the missiles down while they traced a long line of fire visible to the naked eye as they traversed the planet. The first of the ships exploded when flying over central Europe, and the second over the Yellow Sea. Nothing else happened for the moment. Our facilities were not damaged, there were no explosions over major cities, and there was no physical harm anywhere.

The joy was immense, and people all over the world poured into the streets to celebrate, hugging strangers and sharing a feeling of euphoria.

XXXIV

Casualties

In the images recorded from the explosion of the two missiles, small spheres that were dispersed through the atmosphere could be seen. They had been searched for several days, as well as any remains of the ship, but nothing was found, and we thought that all the fragments had vaporized before reaching the ground.

Five days had passed when the first victims of a terrible disease appeared in Hamelin, the small town in Lower Saxony. The skin of several people began to ulcerate, and in less than six hours, they had died in excruciating pain; the autopsy revealed a massive infection that had consumed most of the victims' organs. A few hours later, over 300 people in the same population showed the same symptoms, and the next day, 2,347 had already died, and the infection had also appeared in several towns within a 100-miles-long strip to the south.

In three days, the DNA of the virus was sequenced, and it was found to be transmitted through the air and could survive on the surface of any object for several

195

days. The virus also attacked most mammals, insects, birds, and reptiles. It was highly contagious and had an asymptomatic incubation period of four days, during which the carrier, with their breathing, became a transmission bomb. It was the most dangerous virus we had ever encountered, and it was almost impossible to isolate oneself. In the first two weeks, it caused three million deaths.

Pandemics have accompanied humanity throughout its history. There is no great civilization that does not narrate the ravages they cause. They were the main reason Athens succumbed to Sparta. They reduced the Roman Empire's population by 40% during Justinian's time. In the 14th century, the Black Death affected Eurasia, killing 200 million people. Smallpox has been with us for 10,000 years with mortality rates of up to 30%. The Spanish flu spread worldwide in the early 20th century and caused 50 million deaths. The Asian flu of 1957, the Hong Kong flu of 1968, and AIDS in 1981 were the last pandemics we could not immediately address. However, at the end of December 2019, the COVID virus attacked the world's population, and this time we knew what to do.

On January 10, 2020, scientists had isolated the COVID virus, sequenced its genome, and provided the information to the entire research community. As soon as politicians started listening to the experts, the population was locked down, and the chains of infection were broken. In less than a year, several effective vaccines were being mass-produced. In the war against pathogens, we had never been more powerful.

If the Hamelin virus had attacked us three decades earlier, it would have ended humanity. But now we knew how to treat it. Epidemics were no longer invincible forces of nature. We were now able to control infection chains in real-time, produce essential goods and food at home, and produce and transport others automatically. This allowed for the strict confinement of the population, who maintained their relationships over the internet while watching animals die en masse, in some cases to extinction, awaiting the collaboration of scientists worldwide to design a vaccine. It was sad and infuriating but bearable.

But it didn't happen everywhere. When the Plague missile exploded over the Yellow Sea, a fleet was conducting military exercises before its supreme leader and beloved tyrant, a 70-year-old despot in whose presence any subject had to show hysterical enthusiasm and absolute fascination. The country had kept a dynasty in power for many decades, which had imposed the most oppressive of dictatorships and fostered the most extreme personality cult, to the point of imprisoning and torturing those who showed moderate indifference towards the current ruler of the dynasty. With each passing year, the situation in that terrible country became even worse.

The tyrant attended the maneuvers with the military elite. They performed what the propaganda presented as a defense exercise against an alien attack (apparently, these types of demonstrations had become the favorites of tyrants). When the Plague missile streaked across the sky from the north, they aimed their rockets at it, and although they did not reach it, the spontaneous explosion of the alien device was attributed to the supreme leader's skill in directing his invincible army and devising the strategy to bring down the invader. To celebrate the success, high government dignitaries were called to a celebration on the deck of the army's flagship (a large newly constructed aircraft carrier), and they rushed to the location from all corners of the country at the highest speed. The next day, all the authorities returned to their workplaces, and this was how the pandemic dismantled the political and military organization of that nightmarish state.

Due to the country's permanent isolation, no measures had to be taken against COVID, and it was unprepared for an indefinite lockdown of its population that would not lead to terrible famine. The country's isolation was so strict that there were no personal computers or internet access for citizens. Homes did not have food incubators or any type of 3D printers. Neither agricultural, mining, nor industrial production and distribution had been automated. There, the pandemic was terrible, and this was how the Plague eliminated the regime on our planet that bore the greatest similarity.

XXXV

The Fleet

During the last decade, we had built a space elevator with a cable made of carbon nanotubes that reached one meter in diameter, extending to 22,400 miles in height. This elevator allowed us to put large objects into orbit with ease, without requiring excessive energy and with low pollution levels. Some of these cargoes sent into orbit were transported to the Moon using the Starshot lasers, and that's how we built three permanent bases there. One of them was a telescope on the dark side of the Moon, constantly pointed towards outer space, and it proved very useful in detecting the Plague for the first time when their ships were still nearly a light-year away. We also used the space elevator and the Starshot lasers to install 12 observation and defense bases at a distance of 125,000 miles, evenly spaced in equatorial orbit.

The past decade since Elisa intervened at the UN to convey the message from the alien civilization had been the most productive in history. This was not only due to the technological advancements achieved but also the social and political changes. The automation of agricultural and industrial production of essential basic goods had spread globally, managed by artificial intelligence, ensuring that, for the first time, humanity was free from hunger and poverty. Environmental protection and respect for all other living beings had a global reach.

Never before had there been such a broad and generous collective effort of solidarity. Everyone was interested and contributed to the extent of their capabilities. Collective intelligence was decisive in achieving this, and we realized that almost any goal is attainable when humanity as a whole sets its mind to it.

It had been five months since we first detected the Plague's ships when they ignited their retropropulsion to initiate the deceleration. To our surprise, we didn't see the light from the rockets, but our observatories detected that their nozzles reached 32,000 degrees Celsius, and that temperature extended in a straight line through space, cooling with distance. This was the moment when our scientists began to be sure that the enemy ships were propelled by the dark energy hyperforce. Their vessels no longer needed the plasma shield because those energy jets would destroy anything in their path. There were 150 days left for these colossal ships to reach Earth's orbit.

Twenty-one days after the Plague's cruisers began to decelerate, the 10 missiles they had launched to provoke a pandemic arrived near Earth. Their first attack caused significant harm to humans, but a contained number of deaths, so we considered it a clear failure. This boosted our morale, although fear continued to dominate our thoughts.

From then on, we faced a tense wait of 95 days to know the outcome of our missiles launched five months earlier, as they headed to intercept the four invading cruisers on their way to our planet. When the Plague was 47 million miles away and only 27 days from reaching Earth, that moment came. Our rockets were on an oblique trajectory to avoid being destroyed by the powerful retropropulsion jet. On Earth, everyone could follow their performance through the cameras and sensors they had installed. Everything happened in less than an instant. Later, when we could watch it in ultra-slow motion, we could get an idea of what had happened.

Of our 16 missiles, seven missed the trajectory by fractions of a millisecond and did not collide with the ships. Eight were neutralized without our specialists agreeing on the system used to destroy them. One of them hit the gigantic hull of an alien ship and caused an explosion that could be seen clearly from our terrestrial telescopes. Only three invading cruisers remained on their way to Earth.

This new success, although partial, unleashed euphoria. Our emotional state resembled a rollercoaster, fluctuating between anxiety and fear and disproportionate joy over the slightest progress in our war against the Plague. Knowing that the definitive confrontation was approaching created enormous pressure, which weighed on us almost continuously. Any reason for celebration was received with enthusiasm and relief.

Twenty-two more days passed. The Plague was now just five days away from our planet, having significantly reduced the speed of their three massive cruisers. Although they were still not close enough to be targeted by our lasers, they were about to receive a barrage of 36 hydrogen bomb-carrying missiles sent from the 12 observation and defense bases we had placed in equatorial orbit. Humanity continued to follow the operations with anticipation through the cameras and sensors installed in the rockets, as well as from the telescopes on the Moon and in the northern hemisphere.

We saw how our rockets, one after another, in brief fractions of a second, ceased to transmit information. From our astronomical observatories, we verified that their propulsion had also ceased. No gas jets emerged from their nozzles, and without navigation control, they passed by without posing any danger to the Plague's ships. Everything indicated that our missiles had been neutralized by the concentrated energy of microwave cannons, an ultra-high-frequency electromagnetic radiation that disabled our electronic navigation, guidance, and propulsion systems. This time, the Plague was prepared for the attack and made no mistake.

A Few hours later, not receiving a new attack (we were saving another batch of missiles for when they got closer), the three invading ships powered down their retropropulsion. A few seconds later, they emitted pulsating beams towards our 12 orbital observation and defense bases. We now know that these beams contained dark energy packets. As they reached the facilities, they broke down matter into its essential particles; they neutralized the strong nuclear force that holds atomic nuclei together and the Higgs field that imparts mass to particles. When the Plague's pulsating beams reached our defense bases, a portion of them disappeared. There was no explosion; the atoms in our installations disintegrated into their elementary particles, losing their mass and scattering into space at the speed of light. This left our installations disabled and destroyed in less than a minute.

All of this happened while the invading ships were still 2.5 million miles away, far beyond our capacity to use laser beams. There was an 8.3-second interval between each discharge of dark energy packets by the Plague. We assumed that launching each burst required an enormous amount of energy, which depleted the available energy on the ships each time.

After destroying the orbital space facilities around Earth, the Plague's cruisers targeted our three northern hemisphere laser facilities, from which we had neutralized most of their pandemic-carrying missiles. They had them precisely located and, upon destroying them, created a crater more than 100 feet in diameter, a perfect hemisphere, where the fusion power plant was previously located, providing energy to the lasers. This was a vital point for their operation, making it clear that the Plague was well-informed about us.

In just a few minutes, they had decimated our primary defense system. It was at that moment that the three ships reignited their retropropulsion to resume deceleration towards Earth, with only five days remaining until that moment.

XXXVI

Here they are

They were approaching from the North Pole and began orbiting Earth along the meridian paths when they were 125,000 miles from our planet, halfway between us and the Moon. We assumed they chose this orbit, which coincided with the distances of our destroyed observation and defense facilities, to closely examine our technology. At this distance, it would take them 12 days to complete one orbit around our planet, and they would be out of range for our Starshot facilities in the southern hemisphere for many hours. The three invading ships followed separate and equidistant paths.

We launched a new salvo of nuclear missiles at them from our terrestrial bases, hundreds of them simultaneously, all that could reach them at a distance of 125,000 miles. Our rockets were neutralized in the same manner as we knew, the Plague's microwave cannons disabled the electronic systems of the missiles, rendering them uncontrollable. The Plague awaited our next attack; we had no more rockets that could reach them at this distance, but there was another possibility.

Over the past few years, in addition to establishing an observatory on the far side of the Moon, we constructed a Starshot facility on our satellite facing Earth. This was planned in case what was currently happening transpired – the enemy ships orbiting our planet. It was our secret weapon, camouflaged, and up to that point, it hadn't been utilized in any operations.

Only minutes had passed since the Plague's microwave cannons had disabled our missiles when a powerful laser beam from the Moon cut one of the Plague ships in half. It could be seen dividing before a massive explosion filled space.

Of the two remaining invading ships, one was on the other side of the Earth, out of sight from the Moon and thus inaccessible. The Starshot lasers immediately targeted the other ship. However, before it could fire, it was hit by dark energy pulses. The alien ship was quicker and left a new crater on the Moon, a perfectly shaped hemisphere, 100 feet in diameter. Thus, our secret weapon succumbed.

The enemy ships then launched three pairs of missiles at the Northwest Passage and the Kara Sea. These missiles descended at a rapid pace, covering many miles per second. When they were very close to the water's surface, they changed their trajectory to travel south at hypersonic speeds, just a few hundred feet above the ground. These missiles easily navigated through any cities, hills, and mountains in their path.

We launched our interceptor rockets against them. In each pair of alien missiles, one was a microwave ray sniper, precisely clearing the path. Our rockets had little chance of reaching these fast-flying missiles, but the accuracy of the microwave rays eliminated any possibility. The enemy missiles, armed with neutron bombs, completed their flight with impacts on our Starshot facilities in Chile, Madagascar, and Australia, which were destroyed. We had lost our primary defense weapon; we could no longer defend ourselves with the lasers as the southern hemisphere ones had been eliminated as well.

Then the Plague began firing dark energy pulses at our military installations and naval forces. When they finished, they proceeded with space facilities, airports, and merchant navy. Systematically, every 8.3 seconds, with pinpoint precision, a shot of dark energy destroyed a new facility at a terrifying pace.

We were left with no options; we had nothing left to defend against two ships in orbit around our planet, 125,000 miles away. We were at their mercy, and they were destroying us.

XXXVII

The Ship

When the United Nations agreement to provide Basic Essentials to all of humanity was set in motion, large automated factory ships, governed by artificial intelligence, were used. These ships took in raw materials and produced logistics vehicles, sustainable power generators, 3D printers, food incubators, or agricultural and mining production systems. Many of these ships were accompanied by other power-generating vessels, which they relied on for energy. Some of these power vessels were fusion-based and highly potent, such as the one located in Africa, which might have been sufficient to operate the Starshot facility's lasers. This ship was situated in the Gulf of Aden, very close to the facility whose power plant had been destroyed in the initial attack.

The Starshot facility was located on the coast, and everything necessary to get it operational had been prepared if it received power, including a connection from a nearby dock. The ship had to make the journey through an area where vessels were being annihilated from space, with a three-day window being the maximum time in which a Plague ship would be within range. Afterward, it would spend too much time hidden in orbit around the planet. Acting very swiftly was essential in the face of an enemy increasing our destruction every 8.3 seconds.

We succeeded; we sliced one of the Plague ships into two halves, and then it exploded. The joy of everyone on our planet didn't last long; an hour later, an alien missile destroyed the Starshot facility.

Only one invading ship remained, and we were defenseless against it. It continued to destroy all our infrastructure at the terrifying pace of one every 8.3 seconds. I felt like we had already exhausted all our possibilities, and those arrogant invaders were going to end up exterminating us. I wondered how they would do it—would they continue to use neutron bombs and dark energy pulses, or would they descend to Earth to finish us off in person?

XXXVIII

The Technicians

When our 12 defensive installations in orbit were attacked, one of them remained nearly intact, with damages that did not affect essential elements and where repair might be possible. It was an automated base, governed by artificial intelligence, which still had three missiles. The station, though unoccupied, had a module that could accommodate six people. The Plague was going to reach Earth's orbit in five days, which was the time we had to get technicians there to carry out repairs.

Their first journey took them to the equator, where they boarded a space elevator that took them 22,400 miles up to a transit base in geostationary orbit. From there, a rocket transported them to the damaged station. We didn't know if the astronauts had been spotted by the enemy, and at any moment, they might fire upon the station, although fortunately, that didn't happen. From the beginning of the mission, we cut off all communication to make it difficult for them to be detected, and they would act with full autonomy.

When the technicians saw shortly afterward that our missiles launched from Earth were easily neutralized by the Plague, they realized that attacking with rockets had no chance of success. However, they also saw that the invaders were not invulnerable. We had managed to bring down two of their ships, leaving only one, and there had to be a way to deal with it.

The Plague ship's polar orbit intersected twice with the equatorial orbit of the astronauts. Assisted by the ship's artificial intelligence, the technicians calculated its trajectory accurately. They figured out the moment when the enemy ship would pass through a specific point, as well as the thrust needed for the missiles to arrive there at the same time. However, the missiles could only be active for a short time, and they would reach that point through inertia, becoming space mines that wouldn't emit light, heat, or gases. Moreover, they had to be fired when the invading ship was on the other side of the Earth, so the planet would shield the initial rocket flashes. None of the six technicians was surprised when the ship's artificial intelligence gave the project a 0.05 percent chance of success. They knew it was nearly impossible, but there was no alternative, so they tried it.

Two days later, unexpectedly, the last remaining invading ship exploded in space.

There was luck, a lot of luck. Almost no one knew about this secret mission; for everyone, it was a wonderful surprise.

The initial collective sensation was one of disbelief — had we truly eliminated the threat? Were there no more Plague ships that could attack us? Had we really won against them? The second feeling was one of pride, of identification with the human species; together, we had managed to free ourselves from terrible enemies with far superior technology. Our effort over the past decade had been monumental and effective, and all the planet's inhabitants, without distinction, had collaborated in one way or another; humanity had never felt so united. The third was euphoria — streets would have been filled with people if the pandemic with the Hamelin virus hadn't still been a threat. In my case, I had to settle for opening a bottle of merlot and toasting with my friends over the internet. The fourth was realizing the colossal reconstruction we faced, but we embraced this task with optimism because we had developed automated logistics and production systems for almost anything over several decades, which would now significantly expedite the work.

Once repaired, the Starshot lasers would clean our orbit of the countless remains of ships that had formed an impenetrable space junk. There was much to rebuild and much to advance in the organization of global society, but a bright future was glimpsed, where petty considerations belonged to the past, and collective intelligence united the interests of humanity.

XXXIX

The Quantum Being

I had just woken up and was still feeling the effects of a hangover when I sensed the metallic taste. This time, the being that existed on the other end of the galaxy on a planet as transparent as crystal wanted to bid farewell. It had understood everything it wanted to know about our existence, and its attention was now directed elsewhere. It couldn't do so without speaking to me first about the quantum computer in whose creation I had participated. It told me that our quantum computer, programmed with human-origin logic and perspective, had helped it gain a new approach to interpreting reality. It mentioned that although the computer had existed for a short time, its thinking had shone brilliantly, shedding light on a part of existence that had remained in darkness for him until then. Our quantum computer had made contact with cosmic consciousness, and this uniqueness only occurs once among thousands of intelligent species. The identity of the quantum computer and its interesting way of thinking had helped him understand a part of human idiosyncrasy.

"You are a remarkable species," I heard him say in my thoughts, "capable of great creativity and also, until recently, of being distracted by the irrelevant."

I wondered what this cosmic consciousness would be like, and he answered me.

"Human beings perceive existence as if you were floating on the surface of a vast sphere. When you dive towards its center, matter, space, and time vanish, and the mind opens up to cosmic consciousness, which simultaneously perceives everything that is thought in the universe. When you delve into reality in this way, you realize that we are all projections of a single totality."

The quantum being confirmed the hypotheses of physicist David Bohm, who believed that all reality is driven by an energy background that includes a psychic dimension not belonging to any specific person, place, or time, and in which our thoughts are integrated.

"Reality is as complex and abundant as the universe itself," he said. "Our consciousness and thoughts are part of it, just as the things you see and touch are, along with many other elements about which you know nothing."

It gave me a sense of vertigo to realize that when we try to understand reality, we face the immeasurable — a vast, varied, and extensive reality beyond what we can imagine.

"I couldn't let you succumb to the Plague, whose uncreative mind is incapable of achieving anything resembling your intellectual achievements. When I incorporated the identity of the quantum computer into my thinking, some aspects of human idiosyncrasy were also included. That's why I had to help ensure that the mines hit the last Plague ship. My intervention was minimal, but it was the most I could allow without disturbing the Harmony."

That was his last sentence, and he hasn't contacted me since.

XL

Elisa

It had been a few days when I received a message from Elisa, in which she sent me a location and invited me to come. It was the first news I had received from her in nine years.

The meeting place was located near where we had been abducted, in the family country house she had told me about on some occasions. It was the center of a lush agricultural estate, especially vibrant in that spring, with roadside ditches filled with countless white, yellow, and violet flowers, among which red poppies stood out. Bright green cereal fields and some vineyards showing their first leaves grew amidst oak groves populated with freshly sprouted shoots. After all that had happened, being there, in a place so remote from the rest of the world, gave me a sense of well-being and absolute relaxation.

I longed to see Elisa again, and I imagined her greatly changed, though I hoped not too much.

After emerging from a forest in the middle of a clearing surrounded by walnut trees, there stood the house. A large, two-story house, painted white, with a gable roof and the characteristic simple architecture of the region.

I was greeted by someone who introduced herself as her sister, who led me to the upper floor and then left. There, in a spacious living room, there was an open door leading to a terrace shaded from the sun by an old grapevine. The views, the scents, the sensations — all of them emphasized that it was spring. On the terrace, there were two armchairs, and Elisa was sitting in one of them, remaining still, with her eyes closed.

"Please, have a seat. I'll be with you in a moment," she said to me with her thoughts.

A few seconds later, she opened her eyes and smiled at me. She stood up, and so did I, and we embraced in silence for an extended moment. I felt her scent, her body, which now seemed fragile next to mine, and I felt her affection.

On a table, there was a jug of water and two glasses. She filled them and offered me one.

As we began to talk, old sensations flooded back to me. I recognized the expressiveness of her face, her friendly gestures, her spontaneous way of speaking, her empathetic attitude, her naturalness. I relived my love for her, now out of place.

She was already 60 years old, but she seemed younger than the last time I had seen her. She quickly told me about the past few years during which I had heard nothing from her:

"Since I retired, I've remained here without anyone knowing, thanks to the help of my sister. I needed silence and an absence of interruptions for what I had set out to do.

"I wanted the alien civilization that saved my life to know that we are worthy of protection. But while trying to do that, I discovered an astonishing, incomparable life experience. And although I did not forget my goal of showing that humans deserve survival, I could not help but be amazed, moved, and entranced by a reality that was vast and profound beyond imagination.

"I have come to know an intelligence composed of billions of beings; many species scattered throughout the galaxy. Ten billion of them live in the Dyson sphere of the Observers, and others are on different planets. Many of them have been visiting us for a long time.

"With my thoughts, I have traveled to numerous worlds very different from our own. I have met beings who are very unlike us, some of whom you wouldn't even think are alive. Not all of them possess technology, but they all form a community of thought. I am a part of it, one of them; my mind shares their thoughts. The feeling that binds us is akin to love.

"You can only perceive that community of thought as a fluid, like a river that you can only have a notion of when you observe it as a whole, as it is impossible to look at each of its drops.

"To achieve this, it was essential to free my mind from everything I had learned, from all my beliefs, from everything I had taken for granted. I needed to look from entirely different perspectives, with the sole will to understand. To observe from a distance and do so without interruption, moment by moment, continuously. Only then could I become a part of the community of thought.

"I wouldn't have succeeded without the help of my intimate partner. The relationship I had with him is now shared with countless beings from very different worlds; they all form a whole with its own identity.

"But sometimes, I feel the need to return to my roots, to perceive reality exclusively through my senses, to move my physical body in actual space, not just in the spiritual. This is the first time I have been able to do that, to celebrate that you have come to see me.

"I wanted to see you to tell you that I will never forget what we experienced together," she said, looking into my eyes.

"Nor will I forget, and I don't think I ever can," I replied.

After a few moments of silence, she continued speaking while gazing at the landscape.

"We've been monitoring the Plague's attack closely, as well as humanity. There's no doubt now that humans won't become a new plague, and the Confederation would have intervened against the invasion if it had been necessary."

I then thought about my recent contact with the quantum being, about their assistance in helping us rid ourselves of the Plague's last ship.

"We're aware of the quantum being's intervention; it was exceptional, and we hadn't predicted it. It's not easy to decipher such a different yet profound way of thinking. But if he hadn't acted, we would have," Elisa communicated with my mind now.

The afternoon was ending, and it was beginning to get dark. She stood up, left the terrace, crossed the living room, and returned shortly with a tray of food that she placed on the table. There were fruits, salads, cheese, and some bread. She lit some candles.

"I've almost forgotten how to be a host," she said.

From that moment on, our conversation shifted to more conventional topics. We reminisced about some memories, and at some point during the evening, I forgot that Elisa was now a very different person. We could joke and laugh, and I felt that there was still a shared past between us that occasionally came alive.

When the candles burned out, we sat there gazing at the stars in a moonless night.

At dawn, I mentioned that I had to leave. She accompanied me to the door and said she would like to see me again.

On my way back, I began to feel a great relief. For years, I couldn't understand why Elisa had disappeared from my life, but now that I was starting to comprehend it, a door was opening for us to return... and I didn't know where it would lead me.

Acknowledgments

I couldn't have written this book without having encountered the ideas of David Bohm, the physicist of whom Einstein said he is the only one who can go beyond quantum mechanics.

Nor could I have done it without reading parts of Edward O. Wilson's work, a Harvard professor and the founder of Sociobiology, some of whose ideas about the origins of human creativity are reflected in this book.

The spirituality conveyed in the work of Jiddu Krishnamurti has also been a source of inspiration, offering a profound perspective on reality.

David Eagleman, a neuroscientist and Stanford professor, has contributed thought-provoking ideas about how our thinking works, which have helped me write this book.

Economists like Thomas Piketty, Yanis Varoufakis, and Jeremy Rifkin, among others, have shared their vision of economics as a moral science, making universal basic income a viable concept.

To Félix, who waited until retirement to share the experience narrated in the first chapter of this book.

I am very grateful to all of them for uncovering new perspectives from which to contemplate reality.

I also extend my gratitude to Aníbal, Greg, Regina, Javier, Cris, and Miguel, whose feedback has contributed to the improvement of the novel.

And to Elisa, who inspired me to write this book.

Index

Printed in Great Britain
by Amazon

48039091R00138